All My HEART

L. MOONE

ISBN-13: 9781913930578

CONTENTS

CHAPTER ONE

*** Lily ***

Today is the day. The deadline I set two weeks ago. And I've missed it.

If I didn't find a job by the 20th of this month, I promised myself that I would move out. I'd pack up all my things and tidy my room, so Sheila and Dylan could quickly find themselves another housemate to share the rent with next month.

It's a lot more work than I thought it would be. I have to beg, borrow, and steal bags and other items of luggage just to fit all my stuff in. And carrying it out of there proves to be a challenge as well. The warm July weather doesn't help.

Still, I make it somehow. And I even manage to lug everything onto the bus heading across South London to Teddington, where I plan to seek refuge at the White Hart pub until I can figure out what to do next.

My cousin, Alexis, is tending bar tonight. And although she can be a handful, I'm hopeful she won't leave me hanging with no place to go.

On my way inside, I pass by the absolutely humongous bouncer, who silently sizes up my person, as well as all my bags.

"Is Alexis working tonight?" I ask him.

"Yep, inside," he says, before training his eyes on a pretty South Asian girl, who is approaching the two of us.

"Hey, Dean," she greets him with a wide smile.

His expression softens immediately. "Hey, Megan."

It seems like I'm intruding on something, so I pick up my stuff and shove my way through the rather tight double doors, leaving the odd couple behind.

"Lily," Alexis calls out from behind the bar.

She doesn't sound happy, and neither does she look it.

"Before you say anything, please let me explain," I tell her.

She shakes her head. "I'm not sure I want to hear it."

I sigh deeply. She's not going to make this easy on me. But I really did try this time!

Alexis wipes her hands on a tea towel, then gestures at me to follow her into the hallway leading to the bathrooms.

"What is it this time? Had a fight with your housemates?"

"No! I decided to move out, because it's the

responsible thing to do."

"Oh, is it?" she sneers.

"I'm having a cash flow issue," I explain.

"Of course, you are."

"Seriously. I had everything under control. I was doing well at my job, and found a nice room near the office… But they're restructuring, so—This is only a temporary setback!"

"Temporary setback. Yeah; I've heard that one before," Alexis scoffs.

"I just need a place to crash for a few nights. Maybe a week. Until I find a new job," I say. "Pretty please?"

She shakes her head. "Not this time, Lily. I've got work to do."

I let out a dejected groan. So, she's not going to help me after all.

"You'd better call your mom," Alexis calls out, leaving me alone in the hallway with all my stuff.

Ugh. That's pretty much the last thing I want. Maybe, if I can explain exactly what happened, Alexis will understand. She's never let me down before. And it truly wasn't my fault this time.

I scan the hallway, up and down. No way am I leaving all my things right here in front of the bathrooms; it's literally everything I own. Let's see if any of these other doors are unlocked…

*** Sean ***

Three pints into the night, and the words aren't coming. That's nothing unusual, but I wish there would come a point when this shit would get easier. This comedy special isn't going to write itself.

I keep staring at the blank page in front of me. The lines are getting blurry. *Write something. Anything.* Maybe all those comics who hire others to write their jokes have the right approach, and I'm just all wrong. But I've always been authentic. And I won't be ready to rethink my process until I hit rock bottom. Maybe this is the one. The one comedy special to break my resolve.

There's a commotion outside. Female voices, arguing. I try to ignore it. These are the downsides of trying to work at a pub. Even if it is run by my longtime mate, Bob, and thus I have the luxury of getting the back room to myself. It's still a Friday night, though. Busiest night of the week in an establishment such as this. I'm far away enough to have some peace and quiet, and yet close enough to other people to not feel isolated.

Soon after, the door clicks open behind me. I glance at the glass on the table in front of me. It's only about a quarter of the way full.

"I'll have another, thanks, Alexis," I say.

"Oh!" an upbeat female voice speaks. "I didn't realize there was someone in here. Shall I get her for you?"

My curiosity is piqued enough to look away from the blank page of doom and turn to face my unexpected visitor.

She's young. Early twenties, maybe. And absolutely stunning. An effortless beauty. Her wavy blond hair is tied in a messy bun and she's not wearing any makeup that I can see. Her outfit is equally unassuming. She definitely isn't dressed for a night out on the town.

She's also weighed down by an ungodly amount of luggage, and winded and flushed as a result. Strapped around her shoulders, hooked over her arms; there are over half a dozen bags on her person, not counting the large wheeled suitcase behind her on the floor. What is she doing, moving into the pub with everything, as well as the kitchen sink?

"What's your name?" I ask.

She stares at me with a thoughtful frown on her face.

I know this look. It's the *I've seen you somewhere, but I can't place you'* look of partial recognition. It shouldn't surprise me that she doesn't know exactly who I am. She's hardly in my target demographic. Actually, it's kind of nice. People tend to act strangely around celebrities, even rather unimpressive ones such as myself.

"Lily…" Her answer sounds more like a question.

I push my chair back and approach her with my arms outstretched. "I'm Sean. Can I help you with those bags?"

"Umm…" She's still frowning. And still thinking. As such, she doesn't protest when I take the three smaller bags that hang off her right arm and place them on one of the chairs next to us.

"I thought this room would be empty. I just wanted to keep my stuff somewhere safe."

"Don't worry, I'm not going to steal anything," I say with a smile. "Something tells me your clothes won't fit me, anyway."

She reciprocates my smile and puts the large overnight bag that was slung across her upper body down on the floor. My mind is working overtime while I observe her. There's a story here. I love stories, especially when they fall into my lap like this.

It helps that she's extremely easy on the eyes.

"So, what's this? This pub is your first stop before leaving on a world tour?" I quip.

She chuckles under her breath. "Hah, no. I wish."

Before I get the chance to follow up with another question, Alexis appears in the doorway.

"Lily, you can't be in here!" She turns to me. "I'm so sorry, Sean. I know you don't want to be interrupted when you work."

Lily's eyes widen. "Oh, my apologies! What are you working on?"

"Enough, Lily! Stop bothering Sean. I can't believe I'm still paying the price for every fuck-up of yours all these years later."

Lily pouts and mouths another apology at me. She's adorable.

I can't help but smile at her. I hate interruptions when I work, sure. But if they arrive in the form of a beautiful young girl like Lily, it's impossible to get annoyed. And it's not like I was setting the world on fire before her arrival, anyway. If anything, my short chat with her sparked my imagination in a way that I couldn't have done on my own. No matter how many pints I down over the course of tonight.

"Why would anyone come to a pub to work, of all places?" I can hear Lily mumble as Alexis drags her out of there by her arm. "How was I supposed to know, huh? Is he a writer? He looks so familiar."

"Shut up, Lily. I swear to God, you're the bane of my existence sometimes," Alexis grumbles.

It's hard not to see the hilarity in the scene in front of me. Even if my ego is slightly hurt because Lily still has no clue who I am. Fame can be an excellent icebreaker as well. I guess I'll have to fall back on good old conversation in this case.

Lily looks back once and grins at me, which clues me in to the fact that I've been smiling like an idiot throughout. Does she have any idea how cute she is? Probably. She strikes me as one of those girls who is used to getting what she wants, simply because of the way she looks. But at the same time, she has a certain innocence about her that speaks to me on a primal level. My grey cells are already working on what 'fuck-up' Alexis was referring to, and how I might be able to help.

The door closes behind them, and I sit back down and take a deep breath. *Calm the fuck down,* I tell myself. *You're the last person anyone needs to take care of them. You can't even write the damn comedy special you've been contracted to record just over a month from now.*

I finish the rest of my pint in one big gulp and slam the glass down just a little bit harder than I had intended. Then I pick up my pen and let my mind wander.

Lily. What's her story? Observational comedy is my thing. Who knows, our brief meeting might lead somewhere useful after all. And as long as her bags are still here, at least I know she'll have to come back at some point. There's no way I'm leaving here tonight without learning as much as I can about her. Perhaps she'll become the muse I never knew I needed, if only for the duration of a proper conversation.

CHAPTER TWO

*** Lily ***

Although Alexis does her best to distract me with the same tough-love lecture she's given me so many times throughout my life, I still can't stop wondering about Sean. I'm certain I know his face, and it's driving me crazy that I can't figure out where I've seen him before.

I've visited Alexis a few times at work since she started bartending here, but I'm pretty sure he wasn't here at those times. So, where, then? Around town? Maybe he owns a shop of some kind which I've frequented?

He sounds familiar, so I've definitely heard him speak as well. I must have met hundreds of guys just like him in everyday life. Blue collar. Working class. A man's man, if that makes sense. Could I have seen him at one of the local garages where Mom gets her car fixed? Or maybe the hardware shop? No, that's not it either.

And worse still, there's something about him that I can't forget or ignore. A sparkle in his eye that caught my attention. The way he made my heart beat just a little bit faster when he approached to help with my bags. I'm certain that if I'd met him before, I would remember it ever so clearly, because the level of attraction I felt for him was remarkable.

That little kink in my brain is telling me there's something there which I need. An instinct I need to act on, that guides everything I do. I've never been particularly good at impulse control. That's been a recurring theme in Alexis' lectures, including right now.

"…You know what your problem is? You're not responsible for anything or anyone. Not even yourself. You just *do* stuff, without ever thinking it through. And then, you expect someone else to take care of you when you mess up," Alexis rants.

That hurts a little. The whole reason I moved out was because I *was* taking responsibility. If I don't have money, I can't rent a room in a flat share. It's that simple.

"I'm sorry, Alexis! I didn't want to stick around that place if it meant stiffing my housemates on rent. At least now they can get someone else to take my room to make up the difference!" I argue.

Alexis stops rage-cleaning the counter for a second to look up at me and shakes her head.

"What happened with your latest job, anyway? Why'd you get fired this time?"

"I didn't get fired!" I protest. "They're downsizing and I was made redundant. There's a difference."

"Sure. If you say so."

I sigh and shake my head. It was probably for the best, considering it was a tedious dead-end job in the first place: manning the reception desk at a local transport company. The days were so long and boring, I couldn't help but spend a lot of time daydreaming about where I'd rather be… But I know if I tell her any of that, there'll be even more fireworks, so I keep quiet.

"About Sean," I interrupt.

Alexis glares at me. "You can't tell a living soul you saw him here."

"I wasn't going to." I frown. Can't tell anyone about Sean? *Why?* Who the hell is he?

"Swear it to me."

"I swear." But only because I wouldn't want to get Sean in trouble. Is he running from the cops, maybe? And he's found refuge in this pub? That's a ridiculous notion. Though, he does remind me a bit of that actor from *The Sopranos*, but younger, and *with* hair.

"Why are you smiling now?" Alexis probes.

"No reason." My smile turns into a grin. "Oh hey, he said he wanted another drink."

"Why didn't you tell me that right away? Dammit! You've got to learn to prioritize!" Alexis curses.

"You didn't let me get a word in sideways!"

Before either of us gets the chance to argue more, a group of guys in football attire enters, making their way to the bar while talking and joking around.

"How about this?" I tell her. "Just show me what he's drinking, and I'll give it to Sean, okay? Meanwhile, you stay here and take care of these guys. I'll make sure to apologize to him while I'm at it. I'm already disturbing you at your job, the least I can do is help out."

Alexis sighs in frustration while she hands me a clean glass and points out the tap I'm supposed to use. "Fine. But *please* don't fuck up. He's Bob's friend."

Bob… Right, he's the guy who owns this place. And apparently Sean and he are friends? Yet another piece of information that doesn't tell me a bloody thing about Sean's identity or where else I might have seen him before.

I'm still pretty sure it wasn't here.

I pull the pint slowly and with as much patience as I can muster, while Alexis flits around preparing four drinks for the new arrivals. While I don't much care that Sean is supposedly Bob's friend, I still want to do a good job simply because I want to impress Sean.

Once his drink is ready, I put it on a tray and make my way to the backroom. With every step, I start to get just a little bit more nervous. He seemed friendly enough, didn't he? Maybe now he won't be, because we made him wait so long for his refill.

I balance the tray on one hand and knock on the door, before pushing it open.

"So sorry to disturb you again, Sean."

He's already looking at me when I make it inside. "That's okay."

I smile. Gah. I'm stupidly nervous. But I already like him. And I still haven't a clue who he is.

When I put the glass down on the table in front of him, I can't help but glance at the sheet of paper he's been scribbling on. His handwriting is pretty messy, making it hard to read anything he's written. They say smart people have the worst handwriting. Something tells me that's true.

His eyes are on me, making me feel self conscious, so I stop peeping at his work-in-progress.

"How is your work going?" I ask.

He makes a face. "It's going nowhere. Take a seat."

I look back at the door. Alexis is going to be pissed when she finds me lingering in here. But then again, if Sean wants me to stay, I should probably do what he says to keep him happy. With him being *Bob's friend* and all. I still don't know why that matters to her so much. She's just courteous enough at work to come across as professional, but she's never been a suck up. Not at this job and not at any previous job either.

So, I sit down next to him and glance at him sideways while crossing one leg over the other.

"Alexis warned me not to tell anyone I saw you here," I say.

He presses his lips together and nods. "Would be nice if you didn't."

I study his face for a moment, before noticing the flutter of a smile break through his previously solemn expression.

"You have no idea who I am, do you?" he says.

I cock my head to the side and smile apologetically. "I know your face. And I know your first name is Sean. But that's all. It's been driving me crazy!"

"Well, then I'm in no danger of being discovered here. Even if you did tell someone."

"Argh, no! You can't leave me hanging like this. Seriously!" I plead, placing my hand on top of his arm for a brief second, before taking it away again. That was… interesting.

So many sensations. So much confusion.

I look up at his face and find that he's already staring at me.

He must think I'm just a dumb little girl. Flaky. Naive. Everything Alexis keeps telling me. At the same time, he's a mystery I'm dying to unravel. I wish I could read his thoughts, just to figure out if that momentary touch affected him too.

"What about you? What's the story with all the luggage?" he asks.

I shrug and fold my hands in my lap. This is *so* embarrassing.

"Lost my job a couple of weeks back, so I'd made a deal with myself that I'd move out of my house-share if I didn't find a new one quickly. I didn't want to stay there once I knew I'd never be able to scrape together my rent for the coming month."

"It's a tough world out there, especially with the economy being what it is," he says. There's a warmth in his voice which I'm not used to hearing. Compassion is hard to come by in this *tough world*, as he puts it.

"Exactly! That's what I've been trying to tell Alexis, but she thinks it's all my fault. Says I'm a flake." I shrug again. "Whatever. I'll figure it out. I can always go to my mom's house while I find another job."

That last bit pinches a lot more than perhaps it should, and I make a face. Moving back home would be the ultimate sign that I'm a failure in life. Alexis would be proved right. Plus, I hate Mom's current boyfriend.

"Something tells me you don't want to do that."

"I don't."

"Why don't you get yourself something to drink as well. Put it on my tab. And we'll see if we can't figure this out together."

I stare at him for a few seconds. Is he being serious? I literally want nothing more than to sit here and have a drink with this kind stranger, if only to figure out who he really is.

Looking at him is making me want things, though. Things that I'm sure haven't even crossed his mind. He seems to be playing the role of authority figure, like a mentor or perhaps even a father figure, when that's the last thing on my mind. I glance into his eyes and savor the fuzzy, bubbly feeling that he inspires in my chest.

He looks to be around forty. And he's successful enough that most people around here would know who he is, which is why he's hiding in the back room. Except me, apparently. So, on top of him thinking of me as just a dumb child, I've already hurt his ego too… That's a pretty shaky start.

Should I risk it anyway? Should I give in to my impulse to flirt with him? What started off as a pretty shitty evening might just turn into a night to remember. If I'm lucky, that is.

"Okay, I'll be right back." I smile briefly, before getting up. I love how he smiles back at me. Perhaps there's hope for us yet.

CHAPTER THREE

*** Sean ***

Minutes pass and Lily hasn't come back yet. I guess it's my own fault.

I came on too strong. The optics are all bad anyway. I'm damn lucky there isn't some wannabe paparazzo lurking around just waiting to capture every second of Lily's discomfort with his smartphone.

Why would this pretty young thing want to sit here, alone with me, and endure my probing questions and inappropriate stares? The way she looked at me before leaving told the whole story, really. She thinks I'm a creep. Can I blame her?

Ever since she burst in here the first time around, I've been imagining scenarios in my head which are too filthy to confess even to myself. Sure, I've got money and fame, which can be a plus point, but I'm a bastard and pretty damn ugly to boot. Most women are smart enough to instinctively know I'm not worth bothering with before I even open my mouth.

It's this self awareness I have brought to my

material in the past. A blunt honesty about who I am and what I deserve.

Forty years old and twice divorced.

That's a pretty good title for the upcoming special, actually. I hurriedly scribble it down onto the page, before the door creaks behind me, prompting me to turn around again.

"I'm *so* sorry," Lily says. "I had to convince Alexis that you *really* asked me to come back here with a drink. I swear she still thinks I'm a child and doesn't believe a word I tell her most of the time. We're cousins, you know. She really lords it over me that she's the older one." She grimaces and shakes her head.

I'm just happy she came back at all, and I guess it's showing, because now she's staring at me from the doorway with the most adorable pout on her face.

"Stop laughing at my misery," she says.

"I'm not laughing *at* you, honestly!" I protest.

She walks over, pulls back the chair beside mine, and plops down on it with a sigh.

"Okay, I choose to believe you… Now, will you please tell me where I might have seen your face before?" she asks, then takes a generous swig from the bottle of sweet cider she's brought for herself, while looking right at me.

"Give up my secret identity? That seems risky."

"What, you're a superhero now? That's a new one.

What's your superpower?" she asks.

I grin and slide the pint glass around on the table, leaving swirls of condensation behind on the wooden surface. "If I had a superpower, I guess it would be making people laugh."

She leans back and frowns at me again. She keeps staring at me for a good thirty seconds or so. It's absolutely adorable.

"Oh, shit! You're on that show. The news satire show—what's it called?" she exclaims suddenly.

"Bingo." More than one show, so I'm not sure which one she's referring to. By now, I'm on the air almost every day of the week. I guess Lily has more exciting things to fill her time with than watching some guy old enough to be her dad on TV.

"Jesus. I've seen it, obviously, that's how I recognized you, but I mean…" Her voice trails off.

"But you don't *really* watch it. It's okay. Different strokes for different folks."

"You're different in person, though," she remarks.

I raise my eyebrows, almost involuntarily. "Am I?"

Good 'different', or bad 'different'?

"Don't take this the wrong way, please," she says.

Ah. Bad 'different', it is.

"I won't, don't worry," I lie. I'm not sure why, but her approval seems like the most important thing in the world to me right now.

"Every time I've seen you on TV, you seemed

kind of sad? I don't know if that's the right word. And in person, you're—"

"Drunk?"

She laughs out loud. It's the most beautiful sound I've ever heard.

"No, you seem so cheerful in person. It's a nice contrast."

Her observation shocks me. Is that so? She thinks I'm *cheerful,* in person? I'm a miserable bastard most of the time. That's basically my shtick.

"I've built a career on being a grumpy sod on stage. Please don't tell me I'll be out of a job too now?" I ask.

"Okay. I won't. I'm sure you can still be plenty grumpy once you put your mind to it."

The girl is funny too, I'll give her that.

And she's grinning widely at me. Like she has no idea what I *really* want from her.

I love to make people laugh, obviously, that's why I got into comedy. Making *her* laugh is my new calling. And at the same time, I want her naked and spread across my lap and talking dirty to me. Neither of us deserve that, though—she can do so much better than me.

"What's wrong?" she asks. She really has no clue.

She's an angel. I'm such a pervert.

"That's quite enough about me," I say. "Back to you. What can be done about your housing situation?"

She presses her lips together and shrugs. "Alexis made it very clear that she's not going to help me out this time, so… I guess I'll call a few friends?"

"Okay."

"Right." She takes her phone out of her pocket and starts to scroll through her contacts while I watch in silence. While she does this, the little furrow in her brow deepens. It's got to be humiliating for her to ask for a handout like this.

Frustratingly, I could solve her problem in an instant. I just don't know how to suggest it without making it sound absolutely terrible. The longer I'm sitting next to her, thinking it all over, the more I feel like a filthy cliché. Like a walking, talking mid-life crisis, trying to aim for the impossible.

I've said it before, and I'll say it again—it's a very popular routine of mine, anyway—no one in their right mind would want to wake up next to me every day. That's just a fact. One my heart is trying desperately to ignore right now. Because honestly, waking up next to *her* every morning would be heaven.

Lily exhales sharply. "I guess I'm doing this," she says while hitting the 'call' button. "Hey, Jill! Long time. How are you doing?" she asks.

I can't hear what's being said on the other end of the line.

"Oh, you're moving in with your boyfriend? That's great! Congratulations! Yes, we totally must catch up one of these days, you're right! I'll let you get on with it then…"

I guess that's a 'no'. I shake my head at Lily, who responds with a head shake of her own. One down, not sure how many more to go. As she calls a few more friends of hers, I find myself secretly hoping that every last one of them will blow her off…

*** Lily ***

It's the strangest thing. I was so nervous when I first joined Sean for drinks, but that passed immediately. There's something about him that makes me feel comfortable. Like I'm not sitting here with a stranger, but with an old friend instead.

Maybe it's the banter we share. Maybe the way I *think* he's looking at me every so often. Like perhaps I'm not just a naive kid who will never amount to anything in life, but how a man might look at a woman he likes.

There's plenty of leg-pulling going on between us, but he talks to me with respect. It's really nice. I didn't realize how badly I needed just that, especially after a day like today and Alexis' earlier lecture on all the ways I suck at life.

He's probably just a really nice guy, though. No

way does he mean anything by it, no matter what my heart is trying to tell me. Even though our conversation flows. I keep worrying that I'll say something really dumb and he'll change his mind about me.

Largely due to him egging me on, I try to call a few of my not-so-close friends, those who I think might still help me out by letting me stay with them for a couple of nights, but something always gets in the way. They're busy. Or relocating. Or don't answer the phone at all.

By the time I've finished my pint of cider, I'm fresh out of ideas.

"I guess I'll just have to call Mom," I sulk.

He looks at me for a moment, then takes a deep breath. "Hey..."

"Yeah?" I respond.

I feel like somehow the vibe between us has changed, that a new tension has filled the air which wasn't there before. That could just be the cider starting to affect me; I'm a bit of a lightweight, plus I haven't eaten all day. I seek out his eyes and wait breathlessly for what he's about to say.

It's funny. He looks like any other middle-aged guy, and yet... There's something about him that's insanely attractive to me. He has a handsome face framed by a full head of unruly brown hair. The kindest eyes. A solidly built body, which could absolutely dominate me in bed. I bet he gives the best hugs. He has a sexy dad vibe about him, which is making me weak in the knees. The best part is, he's nothing like my *actual* father, or what I know about him anyway. Neither is he anything like the endless parade of losers Mom keeps bringing home.

He looks away from me, and my expectations drop back to earth.

"I have a place you could use. I've been meaning to sell it, but haven't gotten around to it yet, so it's lying empty. Just as a temporary measure—"

"I couldn't possibly!" I protest. This so wasn't what I was expecting him to say.

He raises his arms in defense. "I'm sorry. Only trying to help."

"It's not that. It's very sweet of you, but…" But what, exactly? I'm in need of lodging. He's bloody offering! And it's literally lying empty.

But it feels icky to accept. All it does is reinforce the idea that I'm some dumb child that needs rescuing. When what I really want is for him to see me as a grown woman… With pretty fucking grown-up desires to boot.

"We've only just met, and—" I stammer.

"It's okay. I completely understand," he says. There's a change in him while he says this. A coldness in his tone that wasn't there before. Even though I'm a tiny bit tipsy already after that drink, I see it so clearly now. His stage persona has made an appearance and I'm not sure I like it.

He's a bit like Jekyll and Hyde, isn't he? I wonder which is the real him?

So far, he looked genuinely happy, but now… I've hurt his feelings again, haven't I? *Balls.*

"You're way too trusting, Sean," I tell him. "How do you know I'm not just fishing for a handout?"

He smiles a crooked half-smile, then empties his glass as well. "You're probably the only person who has ever called me trusting. I don't, as a rule, trust most people."

I chew on my bottom lip. I fucked up, just when things were going so well.

"Umm, so…" I say, then put my hand on his arm again.

I'm grateful he doesn't pull it away; instead, he looks me straight in the eye. Yeah, he's hurt and trying desperately not to show it. God, peopling can be hard. It doesn't help that he still intimidates me a little.

"I wasn't trying to get your sympathy. I just… I quite liked being here, having a drink with you."

He doesn't immediately respond; he just studies my face for a moment.

"I want to make it clear that I just want to help. I'm not asking for anything in return," he says.

That breaks my heart. Because I wish he would. I

wish he would let me do something for him as well, just so things would feel more equal if I said 'yes'. Maybe not as a quid pro quo, but just... Everyone needs something, don't they? Even if it's just company. He looked rather lonely when I first found him here on his own.

"I didn't think you were," I say. "But..."

"But, what?" His jaw tenses, even though the look in his eye softens. Is he nervous? What would a guy like him have to be nervous about? I again wish I could read his thoughts. I'm sure the inside of his mind would be a fascinating place to spend a few hours.

"Okay. If the offer still stands, then I'd love to take you up on it," I whisper.

His eyebrows pull together, just for a split second. Is it relief I see? I can't be sure, because it passes too quickly.

"But we're not telling Alexis, or she's going to rip me a new one."

That's enough to make him smile again, and my heart rejoices. "Okay, yeah. In that case, let's not tell Alexis. Say you're staying with a friend."

Is that what we are now? Friends? After one drink together? I'll take it, even if I already wish we were much, much more.

"Has anyone ever told you that you're really sweet?" I say.

He laughs out loud. "Literally no one, ever."

"Well, you are."

I look down at my hand, which is still resting on his arm. He's warm, even through the sleeve of his shirt. I wonder what his skin would feel like against mine. Would he be equally warm all over? My fingertips are buzzing, and my chest feels ready to burst.

He doesn't stir initially, but then he lifts his other arm and rests his own hand on top of mine. That's enough to make my heart race out of control.

He's famous, so he must be used to the attention. I hope he doesn't think I'm shallow for doing this. For flirting with him. The truth is, he had me long before I realized who he really is. And I'm not sure I can resist the temptation anymore.

CHAPTER FOUR

*** Sean ***

What the fuck am I doing?

Sitting here, in a dimly lit room at the back of an old pub in Teddington. Hiding from view, with a pretty young girl by my side, like some kind of poster child of what not to do during a midlife crisis.

Surely, that's what this is? A midlife crisis. It's a justification, however weak, for the shameful situation I've plunged the two of us into.

I offered her a place to stay. To pretend I didn't have an ulterior motive would be an outright lie. *Of course* I did it because I'm attracted to her. Of course I want her to touch me, and not just on the arm. I want so much more than that.

And of course she understood the deal; that's why she said 'no' initially.

But now, it's a 'yes'. And I can't stop myself anymore, even if it's coerced and shameful and one-sided.

And all the while, she's flattering me. Telling me I'm 'sweet'. Because she knows the game. She's an expert at it.

Pretty girls are often written off as naive and maybe even dim, yet I know they're anything but. They know more about the dark side of human attraction than the rest of us, because they're often at the receiving end of the worst of it. And they know how to deal.

They'll get cat-called, simply for being female in public, often from an impossibly early age. Unwanted attention wherever they go makes their instincts develop fast. While most of us dumbasses bumble through life mostly unaware of how obvious we are, they can see us coming from a mile away. We might as well have neon signs installed on our foreheads. Most men really are pigs.

All this would make for excellent material, if it wasn't a little too close to home.

Because, here I am. Sitting next to a pretty girl very nearly young enough to be my daughter. If I ever had a daughter. Holding her hand and being utterly torn between how good that feels and how very ashamed I am of myself.

And as a result, I don't even know what to talk about anymore, which is a first. Normally, I can't shut the fuck up.

"Sean," she says.

I study her pretty face. The sun-kissed skin of her cheeks. The blue eyes, trying to pierce my soul. The soft pink hue of her shapely lips. Her seductive fragrance fills the air around us. The memory of her scent is going to follow me to my grave, I'm certain of it.

"Yeah?" My voice sounds raspy. I clear my throat, but never take my eyes off her.

"This is going to sound stupid, but…" She bites her bottom lip. It's so cute it almost hurts to keep looking at it.

"It won't." Nothing she says could ever sound stupid to me.

"I don't want you to get the wrong idea, but I really like you."

I can't. I can't breathe or speak. So, I just stare at her. Frozen in indecision.

I want to believe her so badly it's making my chest hurt.

"And I don't want to just take favors from you."

"You're not," I try to say. But no sound comes out.

"So, if there's ever anything you need, even if it's just to talk, I'm there for it," she says.

Jesus. I already can't speak. Or move. And so, when she leans into me, and hooks her arm around my shoulder, I'm helpless to stop the inevitable.

As she kisses me ever so gently on the lips, I can't do anything except kiss her back. I know I should stop. I know I shouldn't let things get too far. But my body has a mind of its own. My desire for her will no longer allow itself to be caged.

I wrap my arms around her and marvel at how her athletic body melts into me. Against both of our better judgment, she surrenders to me.

It's so dirty and shameful, yet it's the most beautiful thing I've ever experienced by far.

I keenly remember falling in love twice before. Or at least at the time, I thought that's what that was. It felt nice and even exciting, until everything inevitably went to shit, but it wasn't *this*.

This thing with Lily isn't anything as benign as love. It's a fixation; an obsession. And I've only just met her. There are only two possible outcomes: either I follow through and get it out of my system fast before I lose my sanity. Or I might as well shoot myself in the head right now. Because to be stuck in this mental space forever would be agony.

With my arms still around her, she gets up off her chair, only to straddle me like I had fantasized about earlier. Her kisses deepen and intensify, as do mine. Our tongues seem unable to get enough. Her hands aren't just on my face and shoulders anymore.

I want to tell her she doesn't have to. That she shouldn't do this. That she can stay at my place for as long as she likes, but I don't need anything from her in return; certainly not *this*.

But I just can't. Now that the floodgates are open,

I can't stop kissing her. Touching her. Holding her tight.

I love how she fits into my embrace. How she tries to wrap her legs around my waist, but can't, because the back of the chair gets in the way. How her hands rest on my chest for a moment, before slipping into the collar of my shirt and touching my bare back. How excruciatingly close I am to getting everything I crave. How she makes me feel like a man. The worst kind of man, but a man nonetheless.

How fucking hard I am for her. Teetering on the brink of control.

She pulls back from our kiss, and I take a breathless moment just to look at her beautiful face. Her eyelids are at half-mast. Her lips have turned a brighter shade of red. Even her cheeks are flushed now.

She's a vision of perfection. And my heart tries its damndest to convince me she's into it. Because I know what this looks like: like a red-blooded woman, giving in to instinct.

It's only biology, I try to tell myself. It's only hormones. She doesn't really *want* this, not with me. Who, in their right mind, would?

"Sean, I think we should get out of here now," she whispers, caressing the side of my face.

My balls tighten in response, and I can only manage a groan.

God, I've never wanted anything more than just one night with her. Even just five minutes with her, because there's no way I'd last beyond that.

"Unless…" She suppresses a smile and presses her lips together before continuing. "Unless you want to do this here. Right now."

Jesus, I do. I *do* want to do this right now. But that would make a bad thing even worse. She's better than that. She deserves more than to get fucked in the backroom of a dingy old pub off Teddington High Street. By a disgusting pervert nearly old enough to be her dad.

"Let's get out of here," I agree.

She smiles, and by God, it almost looks genuine to me.

The way she's looking at me so tenderly. My eyes. My lips. My body. Like she's fully present. Fully aware of what she's doing, and actually *pleased* about it. She must be an amazing actress. Or she's blind.

She places one hand on my shoulder and gets up off my lap. I marvel at her beauty. At her long legs. Her slender waist. The perky breasts, as yet obscured beneath the loose, flowy top she's wearing. Just a hint of hard nipple grazing past the soft fabric as she moves. The ease and comfort with which she straightens herself beside my chair enchants me.

In contrast, it requires real effort for me to heave myself up. My knees ache. I'm unsteady on my feet.

In part, because I've been drinking way too much lately, and especially tonight. And in part, because all blood flow has been diverted from my extremities, to… Elsewhere.

I catch her staring at it. My shame.

"I'm sorry," I mumble, trying to adjust the crotch of my jeans in such a way that my erection isn't too obvious.

"I'm taking that as a compliment." She grins at me.

It would be so easy to just take her at face-value. To believe, every word she says, every smile she shoots my way.

I would be the happiest man alive if I could do that. But I'm too much of a realist to fall down that rabbit hole. Because I know I'd lose what's left of my heart in the process. This girl is going to be the end of me.

* Lily *

I feel his eyes on me while I gather my things. It's putting me even more on edge.

Pausing when we did was the hardest thing I've ever done. But it'll be worth it.

I can't risk getting interrupted. Not when I'm about to get everything I want from him. I only have to imagine Alexis walking in on us to convince me that I've made the right choice. Because once I get him exactly where I want him, I don't want to have to rush it. I'm going to want to drag things out. All night, and maybe even longer.

Perhaps this means I'm getting better at the whole 'delayed gratification' thing after all?

"So, how do we get there?" I ask.

Sean is still obviously distracted. He's been looking at my arse this whole time, hasn't he? That's fine. I know what I've got and how to use it to my advantage. If I can't rely on my smarts to seduce him, I'll do it with my body.

The intense look in his eye is making me feel things I've rarely—if ever—felt before.

I knew there was something different about him. Something I craved. Maybe that's the thing about going around with an older guy. They know what they want. They know how to *take* it.

It's a new experience for me. And I'll be damned if I'm going to let it slip away too quickly. I'm going to make this experience worth his while. Hopefully that'll convince him to let me do it again. And again.

"How do we do this? Do we call a cab?" I ask again.

Sean looks up at me. "Sorry. I'll call my driver."

I want to make a snarky remark about him having a driver, but the conflicted expression on his face makes me swallow my words. He's not having second thoughts now, is he? I'd be heartbroken if he did.

I watch him while he types a message into his phone. Maybe he doesn't want to be seen together either, could that be it? I can very well understand that. Maybe he has his very own Alexis in his life who is going to judge him for what's happening here.

Shit, I hope he's not married!

A quick glance at his hands assuages that particular fear of mine. There's no ring on his finger. Not even an indent or a tan line.

As soon as he's done, I take out my own phone.

"I could call an Uber? If we leave here together, Alexis will definitely figure it out," I suggest.

He's eager to agree, though I'm getting a strange hot-cold vibe from him while he gives me the address. Still, he keeps shooting a few more of those intense stares my way, which I'm going to have a hard time putting out of my mind later. Nothing compares to having a successful man like Sean look at you like you're *everything*. It's like a drug, and I'm already hooked.

If tonight goes well, I hope to see more of that side of him going forward.

CHAPTER FIVE

*** Sean ***

Lily's Uber arrives first.

"The code to get into the building is 9980. It's the third floor flat," I tell her. "I'll call ahead and make sure the caretaker unlocks the door for you."

She nods and gives me a peck on my cheek. I help her pick up all the bags, but I stay out of view and as such don't accompany her into the main area of the pub. She looks back once, smiling that same wide smile of hers, as she leaves. It feels like she's taken my heart along with her in all that luggage.

The silent solitude that she leaves behind threatens to swallow me. I glance down at my notes once and realize I'm definitely not getting any writing done tonight either. They're not even worth keeping.

I know I'm making a huge mistake here. If the tabloids get wind of this, they'll have a field day. This is bound to bite me in the ass somehow, and yet I've been helpless to stop it.

Now that she's gone, I can finally calm down and think rationally. I should be grateful that she paused before things got even further out of hand. We've made out. It need not go any further than that. Before I get the chance to really mull things over, I hear the door behind me.

"Hey, Sean," Bob's booming voice fills the room.

"Mate, I'd been wondering if I'd see your face tonight," I say.

We greet each other with an almost-hug turned pat on the back.

"It didn't look like you were missing my company earlier," Bob remarks, then clears his throat.

"You saw that." It's not really a question.

Bob pulls up a chair and sighs. "These young girls… They'll be the death of us one day."

"Truth." Hang on, *'girls'—plural?* Who is *he* talking about? "Speaking from experience there, old boy?"

He chuckles. "I would have never thought so, but…"

Yeah, me neither.

"Will you share another round with an old friend? On the house?" Bob suggests. "I actually have some news to share."

"Can't say 'no' to that." Although, I probably should. My liver won't thank me for this.

As if on cue, Alexis appears in the doorway. I observe Bob as he turns around to give her our order. There's a change in his usual expression. Like a darkness I'd never observed before suddenly lifts, and he looks a good ten years younger as a result.

Interesting. I keep my observations to myself until she leaves us again.

"So. You and Alexis, huh?" I remark.

He exhales sharply through his teeth. "Yeah. I mean… It's pretty messed up, with me being her employer and all."

Yeah, it is. I'm in no position to judge, though. "How do you know?" I ask. "How do you know it's worth it?"

He lets out a soft chuckle. "I can't really put it into words. Ever since my divorce, I never thought I'd feel this way, you know? She makes me feel young again. Lighter. Happy."

I nod, though I'm not sure how to apply his answer to myself.

What just happened with Lily only made me feel older now that I'm thinking back to it. Out of touch and out of place. The guilt is dragging me further into despair.

"And I couldn't even tell you how it happened," Bob carries on. "For so long, she's just been working here. No real feelings, nothing more than a passing attraction from my side, anyway, because—damn, look at her! And one night after closing, something just snapped in me when I saw her standing there behind the bar, looking at me with those intense brown eyes of hers. One thing led to another.

Nothing was ever the same again."

I guess I can relate to that last part. Nothing will ever be the same again for me either. As for Lily… she's young and resilient. I hope she'll get past this experience unscathed.

"We're expecting, can you believe that?" Bob chuckles again. "I'm still not used to it."

I'm taken aback by his confession. He's actually knocked her up. Jesus. I don't know what I'd do if I were in his place. That's truly the point of no return right there.

Alexis arrives with our drinks and I observe her curiously. Although there's night and day of difference between her and Lily, she's a beautiful young woman in her own right. Not as criminally young as Lily, mind, but it's no mystery what Bob sees in her.

She puts down our glasses on the table in front of us, and I watch as she touches his shoulder, ever so briefly. It happens so quickly, a casual observer might miss it.

But I know what to look for now. I also notice how he looks at her again. Like she's his world.

I've got to give him one thing. He's not a bad looking guy for being in his early forties. He's always kept himself fit, unlike me. Only last year he was training for the London Marathon. As such, he couldn't be further from the stereotype of the pub landlord. It's obvious that Alexis has noticed that about him as well. The girl isn't stupid.

Throughout our earlier interactions, I've always found her to be bright, even a bit cynical, with a razor sharp tongue. If I'm really honest, it was that cynicism which I liked best about her whenever I met her before. A woman after my own black heart.

She looks up and nods at me. "Let me know if you need anything else, alright?"

"Thanks, darling," Bob says.

They exchange a look I can't decipher. Her entire being seems to soften around him. Just as he does around her. It's quite curious.

As soon as she leaves us, I turn to Bob again. "Expecting, huh? Congratulations!"

His eyes light up. Bless him, he looks so excited. He's always wanted a family as well, and it just never worked out for either of us until now.

"Thanks, mate. Guess it really is never too late!"

We raise our glasses. My first sip is too eager, as is my second, but the lingering awkwardness doesn't go away. Instead, I'm consumed by a growing urge to get up and leave. Because I fucked up earlier, and I have to make it right.

Never too late, as Bob said. I hope so, because I desperately need to fix my mistake with Lily. Once I'm done with this last drink, I'm going straight to the flat to make sure she gets settled in. I'm going to tell her she can stay as long as she likes, because the place is going to waste as it is. And I'm not going to do a single thing more than that.

No flirting. No kissing. No more getting tempted into things I know I don't deserve.

She doesn't owe me a damn thing, and I have to ensure she knows it.

* Lily *

Throughout the Uber ride, I've been revising the security code in my head: 9980. I wonder if that's Sean's date of birth. If so, that would make him forty years old… I'm trying to decide how I feel about that. On the one hand, it's been obvious from the start that he's quite a bit older than me. I don't care about the age difference as such, but I do wonder what a man like him would want with me. Other than having a good time in the sack, what's the upside for him? We might talk, but I'm not sure I could offer the kind of depth and perspective he's used to. I might fake it for a while, but I'm really just not that smart or sophisticated.

If I was, I would have had the beginnings of a career by now.

Maybe it'll be best to focus on the good time aspect, rather than worry about anything else. I'm definitely game. Then again, if it's sex he's after, he could probably get it in any number of ways. Do comedians have groupies? I think they should. There's nothing sexier than a good sense of humor, and of course the way he's been looking at me before I left. The mere memory of that is getting me hot and bothered all over again.

"This is it. St. James's Park," the driver says, as he pulls up in front of a large Georgian style building. "Do you need a hand with your things, love?"

"Thanks, I'll be fine," I mumble, while gathering up my luggage and then depositing them one by one on the pavement.

Looking at the imposing entrance, I feel completely out of place. In my faded jeans and peasant style blouse, with my mismatched selection of overnight bags and bright pink no-brand suitcase. Then again, he said it was lying empty, unused. And he did invite me to stay on his own volition, didn't he?

I take a deep breath and hold it, while walking up the steps and keying in the number.

9980.

The door unlocks and reveals an opulent foyer with marble clad stairs and even a small lift. I place my bags in the doorway to prevent it from closing, and head back down the steps to collect my suitcase.

I don't belong here.

I scan the length of the street, but there's nobody

around, except for one elderly man walking his Cocker Spaniel a few houses down, and he doesn't even look at me.

What about that caretaker, though?

Even after I've carried all my things inside and let the door click shut behind me, there's no sign of anyone. What was I expecting anyway, a welcome parade? I conclude that Sean suggested I stay here *because* it's a quiet neighborhood where everyone seems to keep to themselves. It's discreet. If it wasn't for the nameplates on the letterboxes by the entrance, I couldn't even tell if the other apartments in this building are occupied or not.

I begin to carry my stuff towards the lift. Third floor, he'd said. I'm grateful I don't have to lug it all up the stairs myself.

Once on the correct floor, there's only one door leading off the landing. The nameplate reads "Cleary Family".

Sean had no ring on his finger, and yet the nameplate seems to suggest the opposite. Then again, if this is a *family* home, why is it unoccupied?

It's too late to chicken out, though. Where else would I even go this late on a Friday night? So, I try to turn the handle, and the door to the flat unlocks as promised.

Luckily, what awaits me inside isn't a wife and kids I never knew about; it's all exactly as he said. An empty flat. Furniture, covered in white drop sheets. It's surprisingly clean and well-maintained. And absolutely stunning. The rooms are spacious and airy, the ceilings tall, with just the right amount of period detail to make them look classy.

I place my bags beside the door and start to explore the place. There are two bedrooms, a large drawing room, and a kitchen with an attached dining room. And the bathrooms are luxurious enough to be at home in a five-star hotel. Or at least, what I imagine a five-star hotel might be like, since I've never had the pleasure of staying in one.

I take a deep breath and hold it. Am I really going to live here, even just temporarily? I've never even *seen* a house as nice as this. And the neighborhood is super fancy as well. St. James's Park: now that's a high class address. I can't even imagine the going rate for a two-bedroom in this area. And Sean isn't even using it.

Jesus . How rich is he?

I find myself shaking my head at the silky-looking wallpaper. The heavy self patterned curtains. Every item of furniture I dare to peek at underneath the sheets. It's all quality stuff and perfectly matched to each other. He must have spent a bomb on everything here.

The huge bed in what must be the master bedroom is the crowning glory for me. I take the drop sheet off entirely and marvel at the thick, plush mattress hiding underneath. It looks brand new, even smells like it. I've brought my own bedding with me, but it almost feels obscene to ruin the look of this place with my cheapo polyester blend sheets. Still, dirtying the mattress by lying on it directly would be unforgivable.

The more I explore, the more I realize that it's not just the mattress that's new in here. There's not a single scratch on any of the other furniture. Not a speck of dust anywhere within sight. The polish on the parquet floor is flawless as well. As if it was freshly done up and nobody lived here even for a single day. That realization saddens me. Maybe that's why Sean hasn't gotten around to selling it; he'd rather not deal with whatever happened here. A family home without a family; that's tragic.

I exhale sharply and force myself into action. If I'm going to have the privilege of being the first person to live here, even just for a few days, I will do it justice, no matter how humbling the experience is.

First, I start to unpack a few bags. Bedding. Nightwear. Toiletries. Clothes for tomorrow.

I make the bed and hide the rest of my stuff in the empty wardrobe. Although every single one of my belongings looks jarringly out of place, it does start to make the room look more lived in.

And once I'm done with all of that, I take one of my fancier nighties, as well as my toiletries into the bathroom. With a bit of luck, I'll be able to freshen up just in time for Sean to get here.

CHAPTER SIX

*** Sean ***

The car arrives part of the way through my chat with Bob, so I quickly down the rest of my drink and say my goodbyes.

I've gone at it too hard again tonight. Although the alcohol has dulled the shame somewhat, it isn't gone completely. Nothing short of blacking out would do that, and I vowed not to go down that path again. There have been too many pictures of me stumbling out of bars gracing the front pages of gossip rags of the past already. My manager Ian already warned me that if there's any more of that, the network may drop me in favor of someone with a cleaner image.

Lily will be wondering where I am. I just have to imagine her all by herself in that empty flat to know that I owe it to her to at least check in. I have to make sure she's taken care of. That she has everything she needs.

There's no chit chat throughout the fifteen minute drive there. Fred has always been good at gauging my mood, at knowing when to talk, and when to just drive with the partition between us raised up. This is definitely one of those times when talking won't help anyway.

I know exactly what to do. Go inside. Make sure she's fine. Leave immediately.

I'm almost repeating that to myself as a mantra. *Make sure she's fine. Leave immediately.*

As simple as that sounds, I'm not prepared for the maelstrom of unwanted emotions that comes up when I look up at the facade of the building. Objectively, it's a nice-looking place, that's why I picked it. But seeing it only brings up bad memories.

The vicious arguments. The loneliness. The bitterness brought out by our solicitors as we negotiated our divorce. It all started after I bought the flat in secret. Like it was cursed, somehow.

That's all ancient history, I tell myself.

In the here and now, there's a young girl waiting upstairs, adding up the ways she has to pay me back for letting her live here. And that's even worse than having to face some bad memories which reside in the past.

"Thanks, I'll be back down in ten minutes, max," I tell Fred, who nods in acknowledgment.

I make my way up through the empty lobby. Though the stairs would have been the healthier option, I know I'll be shattered by the time I get to the third floor, so I take the lift instead. I pause at the front door and stare at the nameplate. Fuck. Yet another reminder of everything that was never meant to be.

I knock on the door and wait, with a painful lump in my throat. It doesn't take long before the door unlocks.

"Sean!" Lily exclaims.

She looks so excited, bless her. Her face falls again when I don't react in kind. I try not to look at the skimpy outfit she's wearing. She's gorgeous. Why does she continue to tempt me so?

"You're not coming in?" she asks.

I shake my head. Nope. Not coming in. Coming in would mean a slide down that same slippery slope I'm trying desperately to avoid.

"If you're having second thoughts about letting me stay here, I totally understand. This place is way too nice—" she says. "I can just... I'll have my things packed up in five minutes."

She's about to turn away from me, but I catch her by the arm.

Shit. Maybe I shouldn't have done that. It's hard to ignore the silkiness of her skin. My gaze pauses on her nipples, which are standing proud underneath her satin nightdress.

"Lily, stop."

She frowns and looks up at me. There's something different about her. I notice that her hair is damp. She must have had a shower before I got here. Maybe that's why she looks even more vulnerable than before.

She's been trying to get comfortable here and I'm intruding.

"I want to tell you…"

"Yes, Sean?" She looks up at me again with those big, innocent eyes of hers. I love how she says my name. It's absolutely killing me to just stand here and not act on all the impulses I feel.

"I want you to know you can stay here for as long as you like. I just came by to make sure you have everything you need. And—"

She frowns again. "I thought we were going to, *you know…*"

I shake my head. "That would be a bad idea."

"Don't you like me?" she asks.

Fuck. If only she knew how much I liked her. That's the entire problem.

"You don't have to do this. Just… Make yourself at home. This place, it's been an utter waste. I'm just glad someone's making use of it."

"I know I don't *have* to. I *want* to," she corrects me.

She's trying so hard. I'm almost convinced.

"I'll tell the caretaker to get you some groceries in the morning, alright? Just let me know what you need."

She shakes her head. "No. I'll get my own

groceries, thank you."

I pause for a second and just look at her. Why does she still look upset? What have I missed?

"Have you had dinner?" I ask. "Shall I order something for you? What would you like?"

She folds her arms across her chest. "Okay. Under one condition."

"What's that?"

"You're coming in. I don't want to eat alone." Her tone is firm. As is her body language. But I'm not about to fall down this rabbit hole. Not again.

I shake my head. "I can't."

"Okay, then dinner's off the table. Bear in mind I haven't eaten all day, because I was busy packing. And then I went straight to the White Hart to see Alexis," she says.

Her chin is jutting out a bit as she looks up at me now.

I sigh. She's a stubborn one. Knows exactly what to say to get her way. "Fine! But that's it. Dinner."

"Fine." Her expression softens again as she steps aside. "Please, come in."

* Lily *

Sean's change in behavior is baffling. Everything was going swimmingly back at the White Hart. He seemed so into it. Into *me*. And now…

It's the Jekyll and Hyde thing again, even if I can't think of what I might have done to hurt his feelings this time. Or maybe it's just this place and whatever past it represents?

Something must have happened here which soured his mood. If that's the case, then I'll do my best to overwrite those bad memories with a few good ones. At least I've got him through the door now. There's still hope.

I let him lead the way as we walk into the drawing room. I hadn't removed the white sheets from the furniture in here yet. It looks eerie. Like an abandoned movie set. Or a very pretty haunted house. He sits down on one of the covered sofas and takes out his phone.

"Now, please tell me what you would like? Indian? Chinese? Italian?"

I press my lips together to suppress a smile as I sit down beside him and fold my legs underneath myself.

"Well?" he asks.

"Is this a bad time to admit I'd already ordered a pizza before you got here? It's probably on the way already."

He chuckles softly and shakes his head. "What was all this about, then?"

"This is about me trying to figure out what went wrong between me leaving in the Uber and you getting here," I say.

"Nothing went wrong. Things are finally going how they're supposed to."

"Not from my point of view." I glance over at him and wrap my arms around my knees.

"Lily." Sean sighs. "What we did. It was a mistake."

"That makes no sense. We kissed. It felt good, didn't it? How can it be a mistake then?"

"It's not that simple, okay?" Sean says.

"Seems that simple to me." I shrug. "Unless…"

He stares at me. I can see that same yearning in him that I spotted back at the pub. It makes me feel hot and cold inside. Like I want to just pounce on him and rip his clothes off, and everything will work itself out from there.

"You're not married, are you?" I ask. "Or dating."

Sean shakes his head. "Not anymore." There's that sadness again which I saw in him whenever he's been on TV.

"Then? What's so complicated about it?"

"You don't owe me anything," he says.

As if that's supposed to be an answer. It isn't, and I'm frustrated again. "I don't know what that's supposed to mean!"

"I offered you a place to stay. That's it. No strings attached. You don't have to do anything in return."

"Again with the 'have to'. I know I don't *have* to do anything. Let's talk about something else. Let's talk about what I *want* to, shall we?" I say, while flat-out staring at him.

He presses his lips together and stares back. Oh yeah, I know that look. That's the look that tells me exactly what a successful, mature man like him would want from a silly little girl like me. Doesn't he realize that that's exactly what I want to give to him, and more?

"Okay. What do you want, Lily?" His voice is raspier than before. Deeper.

I don't answer straight away, I just keep looking into his eyes. I stretch the moment and the tension it creates, until it grows to uncontrollable levels. When the answer becomes so pressing that it's trying to claw its way out of my chest, only then do I utter it. In a single word.

"You."

He winces and withdraws from our mutual stare.

"No. We can't."

What could he possibly be afraid of? Why does he keep telling me I don't owe him anything? Suddenly the answer presents itself so clearly, I don't know how I missed it earlier.

"I know what you're thinking," I say.

He leans back and stares at the ceiling. "Yeah, what am I thinking?"

I try not to focus on the obvious bulge in his jeans which has made a reappearance, because that would make me lose my train of thoughts immediately. Plus, nerves. Being honest is hard.

"You're thinking of everything as an exchange and you want to have the upper hand."

He nods slowly, but still keeps avoiding eye contact.

"You also don't owe *me* anything," I carry on.

He frowns. "I didn't think—"

"Let me finish, before I chicken out," I say.

He exhales sharply.

"I know you must think me shallow. That I'm just trying to sleep with the famous guy from TV."

"What? No!" he protests.

"But I didn't even know who you were at first, for God's sake!"

He smiles briefly and shakes his head. I try not to think about if it's a genuine smile or he's just deflecting.

"You know what I wanted back then, before I knew?" I ask.

"What?"

I reach across and place my hand on his arm, just like I did back at the pub. He locks eyes with me again. If he doesn't know exactly where this is going, especially after the stare I'm giving him now, maybe he's not as smart as I thought.

"You," I say.

This time he doesn't flinch or withdraw. He

doesn't even hesitate anymore as he leans across and grabs my face with both hands. There's no gentleness in his movements anymore. Only pure need.

The starved kisses that follow take my breath away.

"You know exactly what to say, don't you?" he growls.

I smile into his lips. Yeah, apparently. I don't know how or why, but for once in my life I said and did all the right things. And now I'm reaping my reward.

Maybe he's right. Everything *is* an exchange. I'm not just cool with this one; I'm ecstatic.

Sean lays me down on the sofa and gets on top of me, his body weighing me down deliciously as he keeps me pinned on my back.

His lips and tongue keep demanding all my focus and attention. So much so, I barely know what to do except savor the moment. He's an animal. I love it.

I finally slip my hands underneath his shirt to get a good feel of the bare skin of his chest. He's not just warm; he's *hot*. Literally as well as figuratively.

He's a bear of a man. Big. Imposing. Even a bit furry. Everything about him turns me on.

I've had my share of fun, perhaps with more boys than I care to admit to. But right now, I feel like this is my first time with a *man*.

I wiggle from side to side a few times to free my

legs. When I spread wide and wrap them around his waist, he tenses up again.

He was already hard before, obviously. And now… As much as I'm enjoying myself already, a part of me wishes we'd skip this part and get to the finale already. I can't wait to see and feel more of him as he takes me and makes me his.

Yeah, no. I'm definitely not getting better at the delayed gratification thing after all.

Sean carries on kissing me deeply, and I let my hands roam free across his body. I feel every move he makes, grinding into me just enough to scratch the itch that has been building between us ever since we first spoke.

There's no doubt in my mind now that he too felt it all along. The attraction. The lust.

That certainty that there's something here we both need, not just to thrive but to survive.

It's a cold, dark world out there. But together, we're making a fire bright enough to light up our corner of it.

"I want you," I whisper in his ear. "I want you. I want you. I want you."

I love how every time I say it, his hips twitch slightly. Because his body instinctively knows how to give me everything I need.

"You don't know what you're saying, little girl," he groans.

I dig my fingers into his love handles. I love how his flesh gives way a little under my touch. There's plenty there for me to hang on to and I love it. "Try me, big man!"

He kisses the side of my face. My neck. My collarbone and my shoulder, both of which have been beautifully on display thanks to the nightie I chose to wear. His hand grabs my thigh, then slips upwards, underneath the satin fabric, towards the side of my hip.

"God, yes. Don't stop," I tell him.

He doesn't. And neither do I.

No longer content with my explorations of his body so far, I force my right hand between us and grab his package. He reacts viscerally sinking his teeth into my neck just hard enough to make me scream.

"Give me everything you've got, Sean," I whine. "I need you!"

He withdraws from my embrace and just looks at me for a moment. The doubts I saw earlier are gone. Wiped away without a trace.

I slowly lift up the hem of my night dress, at first revealing the black lace panties I wore after my shower. Just for him. Then, I raise it further, and more of my body comes into view. A strange flutter passes through his expression while he watches me.

"I'm all yours," I whisper. "Take me."

CHAPTER SEVEN

*** Sean ***

"Take me."

Two simple words, powerful enough to change my world.

There's that look in her eye again. That wild expression on her face. The same blush on her cheeks and urgency in every breath.

How can any man hear such a call and not act?

How can any man be faced with such beauty, and not reach out and claim it?

The rules of biology, of evolution prescribe it. She isn't playing fair and she knows it.

As she wiggles out of her nightdress entirely, I can't quite believe this is really happening. It is, though.

Am I really allowed to touch her? Kiss her? Spread her wide and bury my cock into her?

My heart says yes. My head has stopped arguing, because the fight is already lost.

I quickly take off my shirt, and start to fumble with my fly. It's fighting back. Either that, or my hands are trembling. She reaches out and undoes the button, so I just have to unzip and pull my jeans down.

"Condom?" I ask. The last thing she needs is to have this ill-advised one-off decision turn into a life-changing one. I'm not Bob and she's not Alexis. This can't end the same way.

I don't know where she produces one from and hands it to me. As if this was always the plan. Maybe she meant it? She *has* been wanting to do this all evening, and that's why she's prepared. It's a nice thought, though incredibly far-fetched.

She licks her lips and watches me clumsily put it on. There's nothing sexy, nothing dignified about this moment. She doesn't seem to notice or care.

Instead, she reaches down and slips her hand into her panties. Her back arches upwards in a most beautiful display of female pleasure. I want more of *this*. As long as she's enjoying herself, this will all be worth it.

She withdraws again and wiggles out of said panties and drops them on the floor. It's a clear invitation, but I resist. Instead of mounting her, I actually back away. With both hands on her thighs, I spread her wide not to penetrate her, but to kiss her where it matters.

I taste the sweet nectar of her pussy for the first time and marvel at how her body reacts. A ripple of pleasure passes through her, like waves traveling across the ocean. The more ripples I make, the more I feel at home.

Everything that had happened so far seemed like an injustice. But right now, I'm exactly where I'm supposed to be. Whether we even do *it* at all doesn't matter to me. As long as I can keep pleasuring her with my tongue, I will feel righteous.

Her hands fist my hair. Her hips buck into me, directing my affections where she needs them the most.

We have no use for words anymore. The language of the moment consists only of breathless moans and those same waves and ripples, forever speeding up and intensifying towards a common goal.

"Oh God, Sean!" she cries out.

I glance up at her, past the hills and valleys of her perfect body. She's already looking at me. Propped up on her elbows, she's observing everything I'm doing to her.

It's uncanny how she makes me feel seen. How she makes me feel proud to do this for her. Because this blush on her cheeks, the light misting of sweat on her body—I'm responsible for it all.

As a result, I've never been harder in my entire life.

It's nice to learn I'm still capable of this. That I can give her the good time she deserves.

I close my mouth around her clitoris and suck on

it gently. She whimpers and writhes into the sheet covering the couch. A part of me wants to ask if she likes it like this. But I already know the answer.

And so I keep doing it.

It's so easy to mistake the noises she makes as an encouragement to go harder and faster. Consistency is key, as I've learned over the years.

Women may all be different, as are their orgasms. But when you find something that works, you don't change a damn thing. You keep hitting that pleasure button over and over and over again. Until your jaw aches and your tongue gets raw.

Because the reward is just waiting beyond the horizon. And if you move ever so slightly off-course, you may never reach it at all.

And Lily gets there without warning. Perhaps even without expecting it herself. As her thighs shut around my head, and her back arches up as far as it'll go, I know I've completed my mission.

"Fuck! Sean!" she screams through the shudders that pass along her entire body. Because I don't stop even as her body clamps down on me.

Even now that it's over, and I've already won my prize, I wish I could keep doing this forever. Maybe she'll let me repeat my performance sometime…

Her breaths deepen, and her body relaxes again. The iron grip of her thighs on my head releases, allowing me to withdraw.

She's a sight to behold, with her blonde hair scattered across the armrest of the sofa. A lazy, content smile plays on her lips. I could just stare at her beautiful face for the rest of my life. So, I sit back and do exactly that. Until she catches me.

"Hey, what about you?" She leans up on her elbows and cocks her head to the side.

I just shake my head. That right there was everything I needed.

She frowns. "Oh no, you don't back out now. I told you I wanted *everything*."

The way she emphasizes that last word is enough to drive me crazy. She sits up straight and touches me. Her fingers tighten around my shaft, driving me even crazier.

She can't mean it. And even if she does, she'll only be disappointed. My oral skills are passable, but the rest…

I'm not eighteen anymore. This body of mine, it's had a hard life. Too many long nights. Too many years spent on the road touring from comedy club to comedy club. Ungodly amounts of alcohol, even the occasional taste of something harder, just to keep me going…

And then there's the extra weight. I wouldn't last thirty seconds before running out of breath.

"Lily, I…"

But she doesn't stop. She leans into me and kisses my neck.

"Sean. Let me make you feel how you made me feel just now," she whispers in my ear, before pushing *me* down onto *my* back this time and getting on top.

My skin is buzzing underneath her touch. My heart races faster than it ever has before.

I guess this is what Bob meant. *These young girls will be the death of us.* And this is exactly how it'll happen.

She's oblivious to my torment. Every touch of hers singes my skin until my whole body is on fire. Her toned thighs straddle my lap and my thick cock rubs up against her crotch with every move she makes.

"Mouth or pussy," she whispers in my ear, while letting her hand travel down between us and stroke me firmly. "Take your pick."

It's an impossible choice. Both. Neither.

"Do you want me to decide?" she asks.

Ideally, I want her to stop before she does anything she'll regret. But her voice is stern and expression determined. It's that stubborn side of hers again. If I refuse, she'll only dig in harder, so I nod instead.

"You decide." My voice cracks and I'm still breathless.

When she lowers herself down onto my cock, my

mind goes blank as well.

Fuck, it feels so good.

She's tight. Tighter than I could have imagined.

As much as I want to tell her, I can't utter more than grunts.

* Lily *

My first time with Sean is going splendidly. After he gave me the orgasm of a lifetime with his mouth, I've turned the tables and am riding him hard on the sofa.

He's amazing. I love his big, sexy body. His furry chest. The way his love handles give way when I dig my fingers in. His thick thighs, which force me to spread so wide, it's making my hamstrings burn deliciously.

I love everything about him. About how our bodies fit together. Because this was always meant to be.

The way his eyelids flutter, because he's too overwhelmed to keep them open. The way he moans my name. How he tries to follow the feverish pace of my hips with his own, but he's so out of breath, so overcome with pleasure, that he just can't keep up.

I love how much he loves it.

And how that makes me love it even more.

Before I got on top of him, I thought I'd suck him off first. I decided against it, because I craved this closeness with him. I needed to see his face. Touch it. Kiss it. Run my fingers through his hair. Watch the furrow in his brow deepen, the closer he gets to salvation. Feel his breaths against my face and his hands massaging my breasts.

I needed to kiss his lips, which still taste of me. Dig my hands in underneath his shoulders and rejoice when he wraps his arms around me too. This is where I belong; two bodies joined as one. I hope I can stay here forever. The only way this could get any more perfect is if it was skin on skin. Maybe next time. Or the time after that.

"You're so sexy, Sean," I whisper in his ear.

I know he can hear me, through the grunts and gasps for air, because he tenses up. His eyes open and he stares at me like I'm everything.

"I've been wanting to fuck you all night," I say. "Couldn't stop thinking about it."

"Fucking hell," Sean grunts.

I love the rawness in his voice. Clearly he enjoys dirty talk. Who doesn't?

"You love it, don't you? How you're stretching me out with your thick cock!"

He digs his fingers into my arse, as if he'll never let me go.

"You want to cum in me, Sean? Because that's all that I want!"

"Lily…" he whimpers. It's beautiful to hear him

say my name like that.

"Don't hold back anymore. I need to see your face when you unload into me! Because I'm yours, Sean."

Despite the firm hold he has on me, I wiggle free and keep fucking him. Harder. Faster. I know he likes that, because his thighs tense up underneath me. His hands freeze on my hip. His eyes snap shut again and his entire body shudders.

His cock starts to twitch and pulsate. It tickles so deliciously, it pushes me over the edge along with him. I can only hold on as he groans one last time and thrashes about, almost bucking me off him and the sofa.

He tightens his arms around me, as if to make sure I don't fall or slip away, and not a drop is spilled. Too bad it's ending up in the condom. If he hadn't asked, I might have forgotten all about it and taken him bare.

A shrill cry fills the air. When we both flop down on the sofa in a breathless heap of sweat, I realize I was the one crying out. And now, I can do nothing but smile and close my eyes while I catch my breath.

Because that was amazing. Quick, but still the best sex I've ever had. I can't wait to find out how it'll be when we're not in such a hurry anymore.

I settle down with my head resting against his furry chest. Everything about this moment is perfect. Then he starts caressing my hair, making it even better.

Until a buzzer goes off somewhere, and I'm forced to get up.

"That'll be dinner," I say, while walking barefooted towards the front door, realizing I'm still naked, and making a quick detour into the bedroom to grab my robe first.

Sean doesn't move. He probably still has to recover. The notion makes me smile. Guess it was as good for him as it was for me…

CHAPTER EIGHT

It all happened so quickly. By the time Lily gets off me to answer the door, I finally come to my senses again. Leaning back on the sofa, with my eyes fixated on the chandelier in the center of the ceiling, I try to figure out what the fuck just happened and how I'm going to fix it.

There is no solution I can think of. We've gone too far. All my best intentions shattered the moment she got me through the door. Taking the used condom off and hiding it inside the open wrapper on the floor only deepens my shame and confusion.

She seemed to like it, though. Didn't she? Everything that just unfolded was entirely her doing…

She didn't have to. She doesn't owe me anything. I made sure I told her, again and again, and she just didn't listen.

Those two thoughts are still circling in my mind when she returns, bright-eyed and with a spring in her step, carrying a large pizza box. As if she's still oblivious to the grave mistake she's made.

"It took me a moment to figure out that door buzzer camera contraption you have there."

"Oh?"

"Yeah, like, maybe in your next house get one with *even more* buttons on it? Just to make it more challenging?" She grins.

I can't help but grin back at her. She places the box on the coffee table and drops her robe again, wiping the smile right off my face.

Sweet Jesus, she's gorgeous. I already knew that, but it still shocks me all over again.

"Are you *trying* to give me a heart attack?" I protest.

She shrugs. "If it's racing, that's how you know it's working right."

Lily sits down beside me, grabs the box again, and then turns around part of the way. She leans against me, using my torso as a backrest, while balancing the box on her thighs.

"Hope you like pepperoni," she says, before opening the lid and drawing a deep breath.

I don't care about the pizza. I like *her*. It's shocking just how comfortable she seems with this entire situation.

Sex and pizza. No big deal. I can imagine her saying it exactly like that, and that kind of tickles me. *Kids these days!*

She hands me a slice. "What's funny?"

"At least let me wear my clothes first," I say.

She shakes her head. "What would be the fun in that? I much prefer this."

"Are you saying you don't like my fashion sense?" I tease, while watching her take her first bite.

"I'm saying I like you even better naked," she says in between chews. "Why? Do you prefer me fully clothed? I'd be shocked if you did."

I smile and shake my head. "I like you either way."

She settles back against me, with her head on my stomach.

"Good. You can have me either way." She takes another bite, hurriedly chews it a few times, and sighs deeply once she swallows. Guess she wasn't lying about not having eaten all day. The poor girl is famished.

Can I really trust all this? I want to. I want nothing more. But fuck me, I've been burned before. And I've deserved it every single time.

I reach across her naked body and pick up a slice from the box almost on autopilot. Then I remember Fred, who's still waiting in the car downstairs.

"Can you hand me my jeans? I need my phone," I tell Lily, who raises an eyebrow at me. "Relax, it's just to tell my driver I'll be a while."

She swallows her mouthful of pizza and pauses with a solemn expression on her face.

"Sean," she says, handing me the phone.

"Yep?" This is it. This is when she tells me she regrets what happened and wants me gone right now. Although I try to sound casual, I'm bracing for impact.

"Will you stay the night? Please?"

I frown. That's not—"Lily, I…"

She bites her bottom lip. "I know, this will come across as incredibly clingy, and I'm sorry… But I've never lived alone. And…" She gestures at the room we're in. "Being on my own in this big place… At least just the first night. You'd really be doing me a solid if you stayed."

"Lily, I don't think you're clingy."

Relief passes through her previously tense upper body. "Thanks, Sean. You're the best!"

Shit. That doesn't mean staying isn't the absolute wrong thing to do here. I just can't refuse, though. I've learned pretty quickly throughout our interactions tonight that I can't refuse her anything.

My heart is still racing when I type a quick message to Fred that I'll be staying here and to take the rest of the night off. As soon as I put the phone down again, Lily grabs my hand and wraps my arm across her naked chest and tucks my fingers in underneath her. I close my eyes and try desperately not to get emotional when she cuddles her face against my shoulder. She seems so small and vulnerable all of a sudden. That, combined with her request to not leave her alone tonight, is like crack to my male ego.

Maybe she *is* being a bit clingy. And just maybe, so am I.

This would be nice—a perfect moment—if I wasn't *me* and she wasn't making such a big mistake.

"I *will* have to go to work tomorrow, though," I warn her.

She chuckles. "That's cool, really. I'm not normally like this. I guess it's been a rather tumultuous day."

I tighten my arm around her and close my eyes. I'm not normally like this either. She seems to be bringing out a part of my personality I didn't know I had in me. I'm still riddled with anxiety and shame, but the longer I lie here, with this beautiful woman cuddled up against me, the lighter I feel.

It's the kind of high you could spend the rest of your life chasing. The kind that will send you into the pits of withdrawal once you lose it.

I guess this is something like what Bob was alluding to.

Lily finishes a few more slices of pizza, then puts the box aside and turns to face me.

"What are you smiling about now?" she asks.

"Nothing."

"Uh-huh."

* Lily *

Sean is staying the night and I can't stop grinning about it.

I *know* I'm getting ahead of myself. I know I'm falling headfirst down the slippery slope of letting my hopes and dreams run rampant, without checking in with reality first.

But I also know how I feel. And despite still feeling like a silly little girl throughout most of dinner, I also start to feel righteous. Like I'm exactly where I'm meant to be, and so is he.

I polish off nearly half of the pizza, I was that hungry. Sean eats only a few slices, so there's plenty leftover for breakfast.

We chat a little. It's meaningless small talk, objectively speaking, but it still feels precious. Because it's letting me learn more about him. About his job. About his life. And it helps make this rather bizarre situation feel normal.

Lounging naked on the sofa with a famous guy I've only just met tonight.

Once we're done eating, I put the pizza box on the coffee table and turn around to face him.

He looks kind of happy, doesn't he? God, I hope he is, because I really am. And I don't want this night to ever come to an end.

With my elbow resting on his shoulder, I take a

moment to really look at his face. To memorize the little crinkles in the corners of his eyes. Every faded line running across his forehead. The mottled pattern of gray running through his full head of brown hair. He's even got a few gray chest hairs. I'm a sucker for the silver fox look, as I've just discovered.

"I meant what I said before, you know," I start.

"What's that?"

"That I like you."

He seems to hold his breath while he looks at me. It's strange. It always feels like he's holding back a part of himself. Maybe it's a habit. The only time he looked completely disarmed and free was when we were having sex. That realization is making me want to do it again, just to familiarize myself with that part of him.

"Lily…"

"It's okay if you don't like me back. I'm a big girl; I'll get over it."

He shakes his head and stares at my lips for a moment.

"I guess I'm just hoping that this isn't a one-time thing," I continue, while resting my head on my arm, which still leans on his shoulder. He smells so nice. Manly.

"I'm not a good guy, Lily."

I raise an eyebrow. "Whatever makes you say that?"

He shakes his head again and takes a deep breath.

"You don't even know me and still you didn't hesitate to help me out. You're letting me stay in this amazing place, for God's sake!" I say.

He scoffs. "Yeah. I did that. But I only did it because—"

"Because?" I love how full his lips are. So kissable. I can't stop looking at them.

He frowns. Why does he look so miserable right now? Is this not what he wants? Am I killing the mood with my pathetic questions?

"Don't you get it, Lily? I only offered to help you because I wanted to get in your pants!"

I stare at him for a moment. He looks distraught. Ashamed. The penny finally drops. This is why he's been so weird throughout this! Why he didn't want to come in for dinner. Why he kept saying I don't 'have to'.

My mouth twitches a little, as if it has a mind of its own. And then, I find myself grinning widely once again.

"That's all? My God, Sean, you're making it sound like that's a bad thing!"

He glares at me. "Well, it sure as hell isn't a *good* thing! You keep telling me what a nice guy I am, supposedly, while I'm here taking advantage of your situation, to—"

I straighten myself and put my hand on his cheek

and my thumb across his lips. "Just stop!"

He frowns again and looks at me. This time there's nothing hidden anymore, nothing held back. His eyes tell the whole story. It almost hurts to look at them.

"Forgive me, but I don't see the downside here. You're attracted to me. I'm attracted to you," I whisper.

I think I spot his eyes glazing over just before he shuts them and takes a deep breath. "Lily, you don't even know me."

"That's fair. And you don't know me. We can fix that, given enough time and conversation." I fold my foot up underneath myself and sit up straight.

He smiles briefly, and opens his eyes again. There's a certain tenderness in them. It melts my heart.

"I may not know you *yet*, but everything I see in you is good. Believe me, I know the opposite when I see it," I remark. "And please stop thinking you're taking advantage of me in any way; that's a bit insulting."

He shakes his head. "How's that?"

"In case you didn't notice, I've been killing myself trying to seduce you all evening! Don't tell me all my efforts went completely unnoticed!" I complain.

He stares at me for a minute, then starts chuckling.

"Well, did they?" I tease, reaching over and running my fingers through his chest fur. "Because if that's the case, I'm going to have to up my game."

He stops smiling and grabs me by the wrist while staring me down. I'm starting to know and crave this look.

The way his body tenses up underneath my touch takes my breath away. I glance down and see that his cock is stiffening up again. Good. I love that he can keep up with me just fine, despite our age difference. That's how crazy our chemistry is. Our *mutual* chemistry, because even though we already did it earlier, I still want him at least as much. Probably more.

And yet he still sees himself as the aggressor in all this! It's laughable. Insane.

I wonder what happened to him to make him this way? Who tried to convince him he's a bad person in the past? I certainly don't see anything to warrant such harsh judgment.

All I see is a beautiful, messed up man. One who saw a woman he liked, and wanted to woo and impress her by any means necessary.

And in my mind, there's not a damn thing wrong with that. It's actually pretty fucking romantic.

While both of us get handsy again, kissing and fondling and licking and nibbling on each other's bodies to our heart's content, I can't help but wonder…

Will I be able to convince him? Our intentions are impure, but that's not all there is to it. I really like him, and considering the level of guilt he's carrying, I guess he really likes me too. Why else would he even care?

I've known plenty of girls who got themselves a sugar daddy just to get ahead in life. He might know guys on the other side of that equation, perhaps even been there himself. But that's not what this is for me. And if my words can't convince him of that, then perhaps my actions will.

I break away from another one of our kisses, stand up, and take him by the hand.

"Bedroom, now!" I say.

He cocks his head to the side, then glances down at my painfully hard nipples, which are absolutely aching for his affection. "Lily…"

The rawness in his voice when he says my name gives me goose bumps.

I tug at his hand and watch as he gets up in front of me. He's about half a foot taller than me. Just tall enough so I have to look up at his face, but still at a convenient height for me to comfortably wrap my arms around his shoulders. If I get onto my tippy toes, we're almost the same height.

One rushed kiss later, we stumble into the beautiful bedroom and get under the covers. And that's exactly where we stay for much of the rest of the night.

Making love until I run out of condoms. Sharing

breathless pillow talk. Caressing and hugging and kissing each other until our lips are raw and our limbs are heavy.

Until finally, he's so shattered he falls asleep in my arms, with his head on my shoulder. And I can do nothing but smile, because I can't shake the feeling that everything is turning out exactly how it's meant to be.

CHAPTER NINE

*** Sean ***

The next morning, I wake up next to her. Her beautiful face is at peace as she carries on sleeping beside me. Though I really need the bathroom, I dare not move or breathe too loudly for fear of waking her.

A whole barrage of worries starts to fill my head. Will she regret the decisions made hastily under the cover of night once she opens her eyes? Will a hefty dose of heartache compensate for my lack of a hangover this morning? How long until this fantasy reaches its natural end? Because surely, everything must end sooner or later.

She stretches and coos softly as she starts to wake. Her eyes open and she turns to look at me and smiles.

"Have you been staring at me long?"

"I…" Yeah. Yeah, I guess so.

Her smile widens. "It's okay. I did a bit of that last night when you fell asleep. Like a fucking stalker."

It's funny. I didn't think Bob had a clue what he was talking about, or at least that his experience wouldn't in any way be relevant to me, but... I do feel lighter. I do feel younger.

After years of dragging myself through life like a washed up zombie, I'm finally rested and awake. And so I can't help but smile at her.

She reaches out and runs the tip of her index finger across my lips.

"I love it when you smile. You should do that more often."

I still don't really know what to do with myself when Lily sits up, and the comforter slides down her still naked torso. She's absolutely breathtaking, and my own body instantly reacts to the sight of her.

Down, boy!

She smiles at me again and slips out of bed. "There probably isn't any tea or coffee in the kitchen. Or milk. Or I'd make you some."

I shake my head. "You don't have to."

She frowns. "I *want* to."

I follow her into the en-suite bathroom like a lost puppy. It doesn't even occur to me not to. Luckily she doesn't seem to mind my presence.

"What time do you have to be at work?" she asks, splashing water in her face.

"Noon."

"Great. We can have breakfast together before you have to leave," she says.

Breakfast... I find myself staring at her naked form

as she opens the large curved doors to the shower cabin.

"Wanna join me?" she asks, glancing back in my direction.

I probably shouldn't. Though I want to. Fuck it, compared to what we've been up to all night, having a shower together seems so innocent and wholesome, it wouldn't make sense to refuse.

"Yeah, just a sec," I mumble.

She turns on the water and closes the cabin behind her. It doesn't take long for the bathroom to steam up. I go about the remainder of my own morning routine still lost in thought.

Waking up together. Showering together. Having breakfast together. Like a regular couple. Is that what we are now? It sounded like that's what she wanted us to become last night, though I have no idea why.

I open the shower cabin and am greeted by Lily, welcoming me in with a wet, slippery hug. That wipes away the last remaining doubt from my mind.

As the strong stream of water overhead massages my aching muscles, my mouth seeks out hers again. She responds by running her hands all over my body. It's beautiful. Even when things were still okay between Susan and I all those years ago, it never felt this good.

In between kisses, she looks up at me with those innocent green eyes of hers and my heart bleeds a little. This right here is the stuff dreams are made of. To have someone look at you like she's doing right now. I could die this very second without regrets, because I have reached peak happiness. Peak life.

I rest my hand on her cheek, pushing wet locks of hair back behind her ear.

"I want you to know that I don't normally do this," I say.

Her eyes widen. "What, shower in the morning?"

The leg-pulling and banter, it's her way of deflecting. So very similar to my own. I can see it in her eyes that she's truly listening, though.

My heart is racing, and rightly so. I'm about to make the jump away from safety. The tedious, boring, monotonous safety that is the single life I've led for the past few years. I guess it worked for me, on some level. And on another, I realize now that I haven't been living at all.

"I really like you too, Lily," I say, my voice cracking slightly with nerves.

She responds with a smile so bright it could light up the darkest night. I could cry, but that would certainly ruin the moment.

"And while I will maintain that you could do infinitely better than me, it seems you've already made your choice for the moment. So, I'll do everything I possibly can to ensure you don't regret it."

"I guess I'd better tell all my other boyfriends that

I can't see them anymore, huh?" She grins. I know she's joking. I can see it. It's a life saver, because the tension was becoming too much to bear.

"I guess so, because call me old-fashioned, but I'm not in a mood to share."

She wraps her arms around my neck and stares into my eyes again, a subtle smile still playing on her lips. "Neither am I."

When I kiss her again, and again, pressing her up against the tiled wall and marveling at the way her athletic body writhes and grinds against me, I am filled with a strange new certainty and determination. Maybe this isn't all as wrong as I thought. Maybe, if I try hard enough, I can salvage this. If I pour everything I've got into taking care of her, keeping her safe, loving her in every way that I can, there might just be a happy ending in it for the two of us. Or at least a happy few months or years. And that's really everything one can ask for.

"Does this mean I have to start watching all your shows now?" she whispers in my ear, scraping her fingernails down my back.

"Nah, my shows are pretty boring for the most part. I wouldn't want to subject you to that," I growl, while kissing and sucking on the side of her neck.

It seemed so innocent. Having a shower together. But it turned into so much more than that. By the time we finally make it out of the bathroom and order some breakfast from a local cafe, I feel like a new man.

Still not really a good guy, but maybe not such a despicably bad one either.

* Lily *

Sean leaves at around eleven, and although it's absolutely bizarre having this giant apartment all to myself, I feel a lot better about it now.

Oh, who am I kidding, I'm ecstatic. On cloud nine.

I'm in love. With a gorgeous, funny, successful man, who seems to feel exactly the same way about me. All in a night's work.

I'm so excited I could scream.

Sean did warn me that he doesn't want to tell anyone, which is cool by me. He mentioned that he's been screwed over by the media in the past. The tabloids can be pretty brutal, which is why I never read any of the gossip rags myself. Nobody needs that kind of negativity in their lives.

I don't understand why Mom enjoys reading them so much…

Mental note: look up Sean on Wikipedia to learn as much as I can about him. If we're going to be a couple, I should at least know a bit about his life. Figure out when his birthday is, learn the names of the shows he appears on. Just regular boyfriend/girlfriend stuff. He's already doing me a massive favor by giving me a place to stay, so the very least I can do is be attentive to him and his needs when we're together. Isn't that what love is?

The only problem is, I hardly even know where to start. The few relationships I've been in over the years weren't what you might call serious. Because the guys never were.

Sean seems to be, and I want to be my best possible self with him. For him. I could really use some advice so I don't mess this up. Unfortunately, I wouldn't know what a healthy grown-up relationship looks like even if it hit me in the face.

Surely, he doesn't expect me not to tell a single living soul, right? There shouldn't be any harm in confiding in just one person… A *safe* person.

So, as soon as I find my bearings, explore the insanely modern and decked out kitchen, and finish unpacking a few more of my things to make the place more livable, I send a quick text to the safest person I know. Alexis.

'Hey! Got something to tell you. How about lunch today?'

We might just be cousins officially, but she's still the closest thing I have to a big sister. And I could really use some sisterly advice right now. She might have left me hanging last night, but I know that her behavior came from a place of love. *Tough* love.

I'm just about dressed to explore the neighborhood and head to the local shops when my phone buzzes with her response.

'Meet me outside the Teddington Family Clinic at 1. We'll go from there.'

I frown. The clinic? Is she sick? I quickly type my reply before tying my shoelaces.

'K. See you there.'

Remembering the underlying reason for my current living arrangements, luxurious though they may be, I decide to hurry out of the house to visit the Job Center near the clinic before doing anything else. I've never found that place to be of any use in the past, but I'm determined to try absolutely everything to prove to Sean, as well as myself, that I'm not going to need rescuing forever.

There's a bus stop not too far away from the flat, and I look up the best connection to the Job Center while I wait. By the time the bus comes, I've got my journey pretty well planned out, so I can relax and take in the view from the top of the double-decker.

This part of town is *nice*. A little too nice. Tree-lined streets with fancy looking houses for the most part. Beautifully kept parks, filled with young mothers pushing their little ones around in expensive-looking prams as well as the occasional jogger, weaving his way past the other pedestrians. Everyone looks calm and at peace. It's a far cry from the rundown council housing I grew up in. Or the rather ugly commercial district, where I used to work until recently.

It's the perfect place to raise a family.

These people know it. Sean knew it too, hence the nameplate beside the front door: *Cleary Family.*

My heart grows heavier the more I think about it. There's a back story there, which is bound to be depressing. I wonder if what happened there is the reason he seems to be so hard on himself all the time. All that talk about not being a good guy.

Even this morning, he simply had to point out that I deserve better than him, somehow. It makes no sense to me at all. From what I've seen, Sean is easily the best guy I've ever dated. And maybe even the best guy I've ever met.

I take out my phone and compose a new message to him.

'Heading out to meet Alexis for lunch. After what went down between us last night, I've got to at least try to make amends. She's like my big sister, after all… Thinking about you. Yours, Lily'

Too much? Not enough? I decide to add a cute kiss emoji to the end of the message before sending it.

I'm already in the process of tucking it back into my handbag, when it buzzes with a reply.

'You'll figure it out. I can't imagine anyone can stay angry at you for long, not even Alexis. Shoot's about to start. I'll call you after.'

That's enough to make me hopeful. Perhaps he won't be too upset with me when he finds out I'm telling her about us.

By the time I get there, I just about have enough time at the Job Center to check out the current listings, which are all pretty much hopeless, just as I thought. I get an appointment with a counselor later in the day anyway. Maybe they'll be able to help me figure out my resume as well as help me apply for job seeker's allowance...

Once I'm done with that, I make it to the clinic with what I thought was about a minute to spare, but Alexis is already waiting. Waiting, and looking grumpy.

"Shit, have you been here long?" I ask.

She checks her watch and looks me up and down.

"Where did you go last night?" she asks, squinting suspiciously. "Because you sure as hell didn't go to your mom's house. I checked."

Is that what this is? Did she show up early to see how I'd get here? If maybe I'd get a ride from someone... Has she already figured everything out?

I put on a brave face and smile at her. "That's what I wanted to discuss with you today. Over lunch!"

"Okay..." Alexis rests her hand on her stomach. It's a weird gesture, and now it's my turn to be suspicious.

"Are you alright? Why are we meeting outside of the clinic?" I ask, cocking my head to the side and sizing her up. She doesn't *look* sick. *Unless…*

"Fine. Maybe I also have something to tell you," Alexis grumbles. "It'll soon be pretty evident anyway."

"No way!" I gasp and cover my mouth. "I didn't even know you were dating!"

She glances down at the ground. "Let's go to Carl's Cafe. I'm craving a fry-up."

I press my lips together just to keep the barrage of questions I have at bay. Never in a million years did I expect our lunch meeting today to turn out quite like this. We walk side-by-side in silence for a few seconds, until I hook my arm through hers.

"So, Sean and I…" I start.

She sighs and shakes her head. "I'll give you points for honesty."

"You disapprove otherwise?" I ask. Not that I truly care what she thinks. I'm using my confession as an ice breaker more than anything else.

She shrugs. "I'm not sure I'm in any position to pass judgment. Because Bob and I… we're expecting. It wasn't really planned, but we're going to make it work."

I pause mid-step. Bob. Her boss. *Oh, shit!* I turn to look at her, but the warning in her eyes shuts me up before I really speak my mind.

"He's… nice… I guess?" I suppress a smile.

She stares me down again. "That's all you've got?"

I grin more widely now. "Congratulations?"

Holy hell, if this had happened to me, she'd have my head on a pike. I guess I can appreciate how that makes this conversation all the more awkward for her. That doesn't make it less shocking, though.

She nods. "That's more like it. Now let's go eat before I starve."

"Okay. But I want all the deets, okay? Tell me yours and I'll tell you mine," I say.

She shrugs and starts walking, dragging me along. "Fine. Whatever."

I tighten my grip through her arm and gently nudge her in the side. "Hey, really. Congratulations! Anything you need, okay? Oh my God, I'm going to be an aunty! I could babysit, or whatever… I'm going to spoil the little one rotten!"

"Let's not get ahead of ourselves. The baby isn't even here yet!"

I suppress a smile while I try to imagine Alexis as a mom. It's weird. But considering she's always been the more mature and responsible one out of the two of us, I'm sure she'll be amazing. Whereas I'm certain I'll be comfortable in my role as *'fun aunt'*.

As we make progress towards the cafe Alexis picked out for lunch, I let my mind wander for a bit. I think back to what I observed in the bus earlier. The young mothers, pushing their buggies along the beautifully kept parks in the neighborhood near St. James's Park. I think about Sean's flat, which was obviously meant to be a family home, for a future that never materialized. I wonder if one day *I'll* be the one with the happy news. Whether Sean and I might...

Then I shake my head at myself. No, it's too early. I'm sure he doesn't see me that way. Right now, I'm a happy distraction. A great lover, even if I say so myself, but maybe nothing more. If I want that kind of a future with him, I'm going to have to do my best to earn it.

CHAPTER TEN

*** Sean ***

Ever since that first night together, my life has become unrecognizable, as have I.

Days on set pass in a blur. I still count down the hours until we wrap up, eager to get out of the studio at the earliest opportunity. But I'm no longer heading to the White Hart every evening, hiding myself in pint after pint of lager, under the pretense of getting some writing done.

Like a moth to a flame, and no matter how much my days at the studio drag on, I head home to Lily. That's how I've come to think of the formerly empty flat at St. James's Park. It's no longer a thorn in my side, a painful reminder of a past which I'd tried my best to brush away. Brightened up by her presence, by what we share together, it's become something entirely different now.

I've barely even set foot in my own place, except to pick up the odd change of clothes and other essentials. Home is where *she* is now. That's how addicted I've become to how she makes me feel. It's a nice change, to *belong*. I haven't felt that way in many years, maybe even ever.

Over the course of one night and one morning with her, I've become so hopelessly obsessed, I don't even think I could sleep anymore without her right there next to me. Neither could I think. Or eat. Everything I do has become inextricably linked to her presence, whether it's her physical presence or just the idea of her accompanying me in my mind wherever I go. Because obviously we haven't gone public with our relationship. Outside influence would only pollute what we have…

I guess this is what romance is. This is what it's like to meet *that special someone.* To have a person in your life who's so very precious, you can't decide whether to shout her name from the rooftops or hide her in the basement so nobody could ever lay eyes on her.

I thought I'd had that before, but I realize now that those previous relationships were just cheap imitations of the real deal. No wonder they turned sour so quickly.

And I haven't told Lily this, not in those exact words, because that's all they are. Words, which are thrown around too easily nowadays and as such have lost their meaning. But I can see it in her eyes every time she looks at me. She knows, and she feels the same way. That's more beautiful than anything I could ever say out loud.

And she tries to show her feelings in numerous ways whenever we're together. It's funny. I always thought I was too difficult to live with. Too abrasive and unsociable and too set in my ways for another person to tolerate on a daily basis. *Unlovable and hence alone.* That's why my previous marriages didn't last.

She makes it look effortless. The way she remembers the little things. How I take my coffee. My favorite foods. The paper I like to read in the morning. I don't know how she knows all this stuff, because we've never discussed it as far as I can recall. But somehow she's figured me all out already. And it's *nice.*

She asks about my day and actually listens. And once I'm done, she tells me about hers, and I can't stop myself from smiling. Because she can make even the most mundane events and activities sound enchanting. Even her struggles to find a job. How frustrated she looks when she apologetically tells me that she hasn't gotten a single interview yet. She might not see it that way, but she's perfect in my eyes. Just as she is. Sooner or later, it'll all work out for her. She just needs to be patient.

So what if she can't cook and almost set off the fire alarm the last time she tried? I don't even mind that she's quite a bit messier than I am, whether in the kitchen or outside of it. The way she looks at me when I get home makes up for every single thing that used to drag me down in my previous life. My life before Lily.

I guess love does make you blind. And deaf, because I don't even mind the rather terrible music she likes to listen to. Or the films and shows she likes to watch. Our tastes differ quite drastically, as you might expect with an age difference as big as ours. She's not a so-called old soul. She loves Pixar and Marvel and any number of things that I would have brushed off as 'childish' only a couple of weeks ago. Somehow, it's the quirky things about her which make me adore her even more. Not that I'd ever admit that to anyone, even her. I quite enjoy teasing her about all of it, because she's so adorable when she teases me back.

However, life isn't all sunshine and roses. I've been so distracted that my work has stalled completely. And the date of the upcoming special is approaching fast, as my manager, Ian, seeks to remind me of with regular messages. After his latest text asking for an update, this is what's playing on my mind when I reach home on Friday night, drained after a long day in the studio.

"Hiya!" Lily greets me by wrapping her arms around me and kissing me deeply as soon as I walk through the door.

I can't resist, of course, but she pulls away from

our kiss moments later.

"Something wrong?"

I shake my head and smile briefly. How could she know? In any case, it's not something she needs to concern herself with.

"Seriously. You can tell me," Lily says, with a thoughtful frown on her face.

"I know… It's just—" I sigh.

"Shoot." She pokes me playfully in the side—a move which I replicate, causing her to let out a short squeal. I love that she's more ticklish than I am. She grabs my hand to stop me from doing it over and over just to hear that beautiful sound again.

"I'd been contracted to record a stand-up special for the network. It's being recorded in front of a live audience next month."

She purses her lips. "That's what you were working on back at the White Hart that night?"

I nod.

"You hadn't made much progress then. And you certainly haven't been writing since," she says.

I nod again. "Yep."

She steps away. "How about I take care of dinner, and you try to work on it now for a while?"

I raise both arms in protest. "It's okay, we'll order!"

She scowls at me, but the little flutter in the corner of her mouth tells me she's not actually annoyed. "I'll have you know that *that* was an isolated incident. I've been watching a bunch of cooking videos while you were at work and practicing. It'll be edible this time, I promise!"

"Uh-huh," I tease.

"Really!" she insists.

"Okay, fine. Whatever you say." I grin at her and she grins back.

"Now go! Get to work. Stop looking at me and getting distracted! I refuse to be the reason you're going to miss your deadline," she urges.

I chuckle to myself and shake my head. As if I'll be able to think of anything besides how gorgeous she looks in the cute little summer dress she's wearing today. And how much better she'd look without it.

True to her word, she does head straight for the kitchen, and soon I can hear sounds of pots, pans, cutlery, and the suction hood. Maybe she *has* been practicing.

I carry my shoulder bag into the living room, where I take a seat against one of the very girly looking scatter cushions she's piled onto the elegant settee. It doesn't quite clash, but it doesn't really work together either. Still, the overall effect makes me smile. This place looks a million times better with her stuff dotted all around. It was all too sterile before.

After taking out a pen and a stack of blank sheets of paper from my bag, I begin to brainstorm some ideas. All I had from before was the idea of a title, *Forty Years Old and Twice Divorced.* Somehow that doesn't feel right anymore. Too cynical. Thanks to Lily's presence in my life, I'm not even the same guy anymore as when I first thought of that.

How much can change in a week.

Great . Now I've got nothing again. I don't have the first clue about how to be a *cheerful* comic.

I lean back and look up at the chandelier. I can't focus on a damn thing. Except the memories of our first night together. Our first *time* together, even. With this very same view. Right on this sofa, underneath this very chandelier.

I can't very well go on stage and tell the audience about *that*, now can I? It wouldn't be appropriate and it's not even funny. Yet, the harder I try to think and concentrate, the more insistent that mental image becomes.

Frustrated, I get up and head straight back to the kitchen.

"It's not ready yet!" Lily tells me, pointing the wooden spoon in the direction of the door. "Get out."

Her whole demeanor makes me smile, because she's really no good at pretending to be stern. That's more Alexis' wheelhouse. Those two really couldn't be more different despite supposedly being related.

"Can't focus," I say with a shrug.

She pauses for a minute and studies my face. "Okay. Well, what do you normally do when you can't focus?"

I sigh and gesture at the fridge. "I came to grab a beer."

She chews on her bottom lip. "Sean."

"Yeah?"

"You've been working every day, even on the weekends, yeah? When was the last time you truly had a day off? A change of scenery?"

I stare at her in silence instead of answering.

"That long, huh?" She clicks her tongue and shakes her head in disapproval. "It's no wonder you can't focus."

"It's not that. What I do during the day… I just sit around and read some stuff off a monitor, and then discuss current affairs with other comedians. There happen to be cameras there, but it's basically the same as sitting around chatting to your mates. You can hardly call it work."

She cocks her head to the side. "Then why do you look so tired by the time you get home every day?"

I frown. "Because I'm *old*, Lily!"

That remark cracks her up immediately, which in turn makes me laugh too. She approaches me with her arms stretched out, wraps them around my neck, and looks at me up close.

"Tell yourself whatever, but I think you've been in

a rut for a while now. Thank God you have me to drag you out of it!"

Thank God, indeed.

"How do you propose we do that?" I wiggle my eyebrows suggestively.

"By taking a day off. By experiencing something new. Doing something impulsive and silly."

"What, anal?"

She bursts out laughing again and hides her face in my chest. "No, silly! By getting out of the house and doing something fun!"

"We've been doing fun stuff *in* the house every night for a week now. I wouldn't mind a whole day of the same!"

She pulls back and looks into my eyes with a wide grin on her face. "Seriously. Just one day off. I'll take care of everything. You just have to show up." She runs her thumb across my bottom lip before getting up on her tippy toes and kissing me. And just like that, all the tension about the upcoming special just fades away. There's something magical about her. Something so precious, I just can't refuse her a damn thing. For once in my life, I'm ready to let someone else be in charge.

"There's a break in my schedule the day after tomorrow, as it happens," I mumble, marveling once again at the softness of her lips. Will I ever tire of this? I doubt it.

She smiles against my lips. "Wonderful. It's a date."

While she retreats to check whatever mystery dish is cooking away on the stove, I can't help but watch her. Maybe she's right. Maybe I have been in a rut, and she *is* the only one able to drag me out of it. That's why I seemingly can't breathe without her anymore. And why I can barely even remember what my life used to be, before Lily came into it and changed everything.

CHAPTER ELEVEN

* Lily *

I might have told Sean that he's been in a rut, but I've kind of been in one myself ever since I was laid off. Every day, I'm applying for jobs, getting a rejection here or there, but mostly not getting any responses whatsoever. It feels like I'm screaming into the void. I'll never find another job at this rate, and certainly not one I actually would want to do for any length of time.

It's been about a week since he let me move in here, and my days have been largely joyless without him. Except for the day I had lunch with Alexis, I've been on my own, counting every hour, every minute, every second until I'd see him walk through that door. The only respite I got has been when I focused on him. On his happiness. I'd spend a couple of hours every day planning what to make for dinner. Or I'd scrape together the last of my savings to stock up on a few of his favorite things. Because I'll be damned if I'm going to ask for another handout. Not while I'm already staying here, rent free, in this beautiful place… Plus, my benefits should kick in any day now.

That's until he arrives every evening, and I forget everything. I forget how I spent the day pining for him. Worrying about proving Alexis right and failing at being a grown-up. I forget about how I'll never be his equal at this rate, because he looks at me like I'm everything already.

This day off I'm planning for him, I desperately need it as well. I need it for myself just as I need it to make him smile.

And that's why I want it to be just right. Perfectly imperfectly spontaneously unpredictably perfect. If there is such a thing.

Sean's schedule has been set for years. His routine must be suffocating him, and he doesn't even know it. No wonder he used to escape to the White Hart every evening just to try and cultivate some ideas. And it didn't work, because that was yet another part of his boring ass routine.

When has creativity ever flourished in soul destroying monotony? That's right. Never!

So, I spend hours on my phone, just to figure out the perfect destination. Somewhere near enough that we won't spend the whole day travelling. But far enough out of the city to provide a breath of fresh air. I study the weather forecast, which luckily predicts clear skies and warm, summery weather for the next couple of days. And, I study him.

Save for that initial bit of research I did almost a week ago now, I hadn't googled Sean. Not really. I hadn't watched too much of his material either, not because I'm not interested, but because *I am*. Because I know that's a rabbit hole that'll suck me up for hours, if I let it. And it does. Almost the entire day.

He's been a stand-up comedian for years, so there's a ton of stuff out there.

But his brand of comedy isn't something I've really seen before. It's not the standard light-hearted stuff you see on the late night shows Mom likes to watch.

It's raw. It's self-deprecating. And at times heartbreaking because of it. His jokes will make you laugh, sure, but with a lump in your throat if you really stop to think about what he's saying. Perhaps that's just me, because I know what he looks like when he's telling the truth. And the truth often hurts.

It's everything I had hoped for and everything I was afraid of. After scrolling through a bunch of suggested videos on YouTube, I come across one from a few years ago simply titled *'Family'*. I'm already nervous when I click on it, because I'm not sure I'll like what I'm going to find.

Sean sits on stage looking even more solemn than he usually does whenever he performs. It's dark, except for the single spotlight on him. In one hand a pint, in the other, a cigarette.

I didn't know he smoked. He must have quit since

then.

"Tell me, how has Hallmark not cashed in on divorce cards yet? *Congratulations! Now, nobody'll care how much time you spend at the pub or whether you've eaten a whole bucket of fried chicken all by yourself!*" Sean opens his set. "I would love a card like that."

The crowd loves it too, it seems.

He speaks of a woman named Susan. And another named Alison before that. *Fool me once... I guess I'm a confirmed fool with the alimony payments to prove it.*

I already knew from his Wiki page that he'd been married before, but he's never mentioned it to me in person. My heart is racing out of control. This might be the missing key. The secret piece of the puzzle that is Sean. Looking at the three million views the clip has got, I feel like I'm the only one who doesn't know all this about him.

"We were due to move into the new place," Sean says. "I had it all planned out for months. After buying the place in secret, I had it renovated, getting the work done alongside long days shooting my TV show. Funnily, some women don't like it when you keep secrets from them. Not even when they're good secrets." Sean takes a long drag of his cigarette and stares thoughtfully at the audience.

"Well, I guess what I'm really trying to say is: Does anyone want to buy a flat? Great location, newly renovated, no onward chain."

The audience laughs uncomfortably. My heart hurts.

"They say money can't buy you happiness," Sean carries on. "That depends on your definition of 'happiness'. Also: 'How much money?'"

Someone in the audience can be heard shouting. "That's what *she* said!"

Sean points out the heckler and gives him the thumbs up. "You get it, my man!"

"I've come to the conclusion that most of what *people* say is bullshit. They say 'be careful; she'll take half of everything!'." Sean shakes his head. "I find that if you're bad enough, they'll pay *you* just to be rid of you. It was a pretty sweet deal; I should have taken it.

"I think I've reached a stage in my life where I'd prefer to do the alimony negotiation in advance. That way everyone knows where they stand. To compensate for having to wake up next to this ugly mug every day, I'm prepared to offer this much of an allowance, plus damages. If that sounds acceptable, please apply with your CV and headshot after the show." The crowd roars. "Everything in life is a transaction. I don't care what anyone says," Sean adds. "In every man's life there comes a time when you really don't have anything to offer women, except money."

He takes a sip from his glass and smiles briefly.

"One of the most baffling things you always hear people say is about having kids. 'Oh my, he looks just like a tiny version of you!' As if that's a compliment. No, thank you!"

Sean waits for the last awkward chuckles to die down.

"If by some cosmic miracle, a woman wanted to have my children, I'd suggest we go to a sperm bank. Not because my swimmers don't work, but, like… If you had the chance, wouldn't you try for something *better?* A tiny little version of *me*. Fuuuck me!" Sean shakes his head and chuckles before putting the spent cigarette out in the ashtray on the little table beside him.

The crowd starts to go crazy and the video ends right there. And I'm heartbroken.

I wrap my arms around myself and stare at nothing in particular. What made him think this way? How bad did it really get with his ex? Could I change his mind somehow?

It's a slippery slope I find myself on. Before thinking much more about it, I type in Sean's name and 'divorce' into the search bar. My finger trembles as it hovers over the button to actually perform the search when I realize what I'm about to do.

"No," I tell myself. "Let *him* tell you. Not the tabloids."

I close the entire search window and take a deep

breath, still reeling with confusing thoughts and emotions. I was planning a day off. A day *out*, even. For the two of us. That's what I should focus on. Everything that came before, everything that comes after: none of that should be my concern.

All that matters is I like him and he seems to like me back. We're good together. Sooner or later, he's bound to tell me everything. And if not, then I don't need to know. Because the past doesn't matter; only the present does. And the future.

Secretly, I hope that the change of scenery will spark something. A step in a more intimate direction than just amazing sex.

If I can get him to open up to me about all of this stuff, then we're bound to take our relationship to the next level. I might just prove myself to be more than a fun plaything to spend a few nights with, but actual relationship material. That's what I want more than anything. For Sean to see how serious I am. About him and about *us*.

Without further delay, I pick up my phone and call Alexis. Step one in my awesome plan doesn't involve taking Sean's chauffeur driven car on a day trip. No, thank you! This outing is going to be all *us*. No outsiders.

"Hey, how's the preggo life?" I greet her as soon as she answers. She mumbles some curse words, which I ignore.

"Say, Alexis… I was wondering if you could do me this one massive favor… I need to borrow your car. No, it's just for a day; I'm planning a surprise for Sean. I'll be forever in your debt."

Although Alexis grumbles some more, I can feel myself starting to smile, because I know this tone. It means I'm about to get my way. Finally, things are looking up.

*** Sean ***

For a change, Lily is up well before me. Considering it's my day off, I'm somewhat dismayed when I find the bed empty next to me. Her presence has become an addiction. One which I can't get enough of, day or night.

But as soon as she enters our bedroom a few minutes later, with a bright grin on her face, my frustration is forgotten.

"Morning, handsome!" she chirps.

"Morning."

"Ready to have the best day off, ever?" she asks.

I pat the bed beside me. "Come here and we'll find out."

She sits down and melts into me with both arms around my neck. "Oh, I see. Someone isn't in a hurry to get out of bed."

"Now that you're here, no, I'm not!" I tease.

She kisses me deeply, and my heart rate calms and speeds up all at once. It's crazy what even a simple touch of hers does to me. One kiss is enough to get this old engine going like new.

We're so in tune, it's insane. Everything I give to her, she returns it to me tenfold. Such is the beauty of youth. Before we know it, she's got her beautiful, slender fingers wrapped around my morning wood so tight, I don't know how I'm going to last.

She seems to like it that way. Sometimes I swear she's trying to beat some kind of record. But this morning, all I want is to slow things down. So I grab her wrists and flip her onto her back before getting on top of her and kissing her again, savoring the taste of her full lips, her eager tongue, the silky skin on her neck and cleavage.

"I could do this all day," I growl, reaching down to curl two fingers in between her slick folds.

She bucks her hips upwards against my hand and moans. "You never know… if it's quiet enough, I'll let you do this again later. *In public.*"

It's a good fantasy. Unrealistic and way too dangerous to entertain, but a good fantasy nonetheless.

"You want me to make you moan like this in full view of the world?" I tease.

She whimpers softly as I apply more pressure on her clit, rubbing it in a slow, circular motion.

"You want me to strip you naked, bend you over a park bench, and fill you up until you scream?" I ask.

"God, yes!" she cries out. "Yes, do whatever! I'm yours."

Well, what is a man to do when faced with an invitation like that? With my finger still stimulating her clit, I get in between her toned thighs and enter her. She's so hot and wet, I almost lose myself right then and there.

In an attempt to slow myself down, I lower myself onto her and just try to breathe. The way my significantly larger body covers hers is in equal measures slightly awkward and mind-blowingly sexy. Mostly because *she* is. She's perfect. Our size difference speaks to a primal part of my male psyche. I gather her up in my arms and hug her tight. She's like a little doll. A fragile little thing that requires my love and protection, silly as it sounds.

But it doesn't *feel* silly. It feels as though I can't stop myself anymore. My hips grind into her as if with a mind of their own. Her body doesn't just receive the onslaught I unleash onto her, it seeks to amplify it with hip movements of her own.

We rut like animals. Our morning quickies tend to be like this most of the time, but that's okay. I've learned how to read the signs to use my weaknesses as a strength instead. I've learned to slow just enough, or speed up just enough to play her like a violin. A very horny, very wet, and slippery violin.

With just the right kind of touch or the right kind of kiss, she'll be singing my name in no time. And indeed, she does. I grind into her, impaling her with my full length one last time, and she shivers and twitches in that same particular manner I've grown so fond of. As a result, my own release isn't far behind. Ever since we did away with the condoms just two days into our relationship, the sex has been even better, more intimate than before.

I could do this for the rest of my life and be the happiest man on earth.

CHAPTER TWELVE

*** Lily ***

It wasn't unexpected for Sean to tempt me back into bed on the morning of his Awesome Day Off, as I've started calling today. It also wasn't unexpected that I was all in from the very second he looked at me in that way that only he can.

Like I'm his everything.

Our departure is slightly delayed, but that's okay. This is *his* day. The whole point is for today to be completely informal and relaxed. No schedules, no time tables, and certainly no deadlines.

When we finally collapse into a heap of post-orgasmic bliss, it's about nine-thirty. After taking a short breather, I fix my hair and make a quick escape to pick up Alexis' car. Meanwhile, Sean will have a shower and get ready.

I let slip last night that we're going to have a picnic today. And to wear some beach ready clothes and footwear this morning.

Initially I wondered if he's just humoring me, but by the time I return with our ride, he genuinely looks excited. And he has somehow conjured up a whole collection of pretty looking bags from what must be a fancy deli in the neighborhood…

"Shall I drive?" he asks, after placing the mystery supplies onto the backseat of Alexis' old VW Polo, right next to the picnic blanket and items of cutlery and crockery I'd already loaded up into their own dedicated tote bag.

"Absolutely not! You're meant to be relaxing today. At most, you get to be the DJ."

I regret that last bit almost as soon as I've said it, because I know there is very little overlap in our musical tastes. But still, this is *his* day. If he wants to spend it listening to old rock, who am I to intervene?

He hesitates for a moment, but then shrugs and holds the driver's side door open for me, before getting into the passenger seat himself. I turn the key and the car purrs to life. Let's do this!

"So, where are we going exactly?" he asks, placing his hand on my knee. It's distracting, how his touch makes my heart skip a few beats. But it's also reassuring. We're doing this. A whole day spent together, just enjoying each other's company. This is going to be amazing!

"You'll see when we get there," I tell him, after pulling up the directions on my phone and balancing it in the center console underneath the dashboard, right between the two of us.

He sighs and leans back in his seat while looking out the window.

"I can't remember the last time I did something like this," he says.

I press my lips together in a subtle smile and nod. Yep, this was definitely the best idea I've had so far. Maybe I'm not so bad at the whole adulting thing after all.

I want to tell him that I hope we might do stuff like this more often, but I don't want to sound needy and push my luck. Sean is a busy guy, so I'm going to have to be happy with whatever time I can get.

* Sean *

It's hard letting go of the reins and trusting another person. But this is Lily, so she makes it really easy. I just have to glance at her face, with the slightly tense expression and most adorable little furrow in her brow, and I know that I'm exactly where I'm supposed to be.

She's probably not used to driving—it's not even her car—but she's not complaining. And neither am I. Ever since I hired Fred as my chauffeur five years ago, I've hardly sat in the driver's seat myself. My initial offer to do the driving was more of a gender role thing rather than an actual desire of mine. As such, it was a relief that she refused.

Remembering her rebuttal that I'm supposed to play DJ, I turn on the radio and start scanning for familiar stations. I have no idea what she would like to listen to. Radio One, maybe? The tune that's playing sounds similar to the sort of stuff she listens to at home, so I figure it's a safe enough bet.

And then, I sit back again and watch the city pass us by. Somehow the different view from the passenger seat of this small hatchback car makes London look almost alien to me. It occurs to me that my daily commute in the back of my car with Fred driving is not as visceral an experience. It's a lot more muted and cut off from the goings on outside.

Maybe I should try riding in the front occasionally. Maybe I should start driving myself again. Maybe…

"Sean, I'm really happy we're doing this," Lily tells me.

I look over at her and find her smiling at me. As if I'm doing *her* a favor and not the other way around.

"Me too." I really am.

Although the pressure to write some material for my damn special already has been growing out of control, I'm able to cast off the tension and just exist in the moment right now. Here. In the car. With her.

Wherever we end up going today, the objective has already been reached. The destination doesn't matter, only the company does.

We chat for some time. About this and that. But

there's also this unspoken agreement that talking is optional. As such, we share some silences. Not awkward ones, but peaceful ones. Well, sort of. Because the radio is still on.

I don't know when I drift off. It's something about the droning sound of the tires travelling at high speed on the motorway that does it for me.

When I open my eyes again, we're somewhere altogether different. Gone are the terraced houses you find all over Greater London. In fact, these green and twisty tree-lined roads don't have very many houses at all. We're in the countryside somewhere.

I know better than to ask where we're going by now, and try to piece it together by looking at the road signs instead. But wherever we are, it isn't familiar. Soon, the foliage opens up to reveal vast meadows and fields, rolling hills, and perfectly blue skies overhead.

And not too long after that do we get our first glimpse of the sea.

What a sight.

The geography no longer matters. I don't have to be in control of everything, I remind myself.

We pull into a parking lot and start collecting our things. There aren't too many other vehicles here, which I'm endlessly grateful for.

The last thing I need right now is to be recognized by some member of the public. I'm usually quite gracious about such things, but this is my day off to spend alone with Lily. I wouldn't want anyone else to intrude.

Only by the time we've already unloaded our bags does another car pull into the same lot. Thankfully it parks all the way on the other side, giving us the chance to head down the walking trail undisturbed.

"Just five minutes," Lily reassures me.

I'm not much of a hiker, as a single glance at my growing waistline would already reveal.

I hook one of the bags over my shoulder and take her hand. She looks over at me, smiling again. So this is what it's like. A normal life. Spent with people you love.

As we head up the trail and through the grass-covered dunes, the expanding view before us reminds of childhood outings to the seaside. Minus the stressed out look on my mom's face, and the constant bickering over nothing that carried on between my brother Jack and I. The latter invariably resulted in either one or both of us being whacked across the back of the head by my dad, who had very little patience at the best of times.

I inhale deeply, enjoying how the salty air prickles in my nostrils. I wonder what Jack is up to? We fell out of touch years ago; ever since my first divorce...

Yep, this is familiar, and also so very different. Today, between us, there will be no fights. No tension. And certainly no whacking anyone over the head for whatever reason.

* Lily *

Sean's Awesome Day Off is going splendidly. I didn't get lost or crash the car along the way, so that's a major plus. And the destination I'd picked out is as private and scenic as I hoped it would be.

By the time we've made our way down from the car park and onto the pebbled beach, I feel so happy, I can hardly stop myself from skipping instead of walking. Looking over at Sean, I can tell he feels the same.

He's visibly relaxed. Strangely, even more so than every night he's fallen asleep next to me this week. There's always been a little crinkle between his eyebrows. A hint of tension in his jaw. Always some reminder that he's not one to let go.

Now, everything about him is brighter. More carefree. Like he's finally rid himself of the silly notion that he's taking advantage of me somehow. That was his biggest hang-up on the night we first got together, wasn't it? It was nonsense, of course, but I've had the hardest time trying to convince him of that.

Once we've set up our picnic blanket and all the supplies I'd packed, we settle down next to each other with a sigh of relief. Sean and I share a kiss, which involves both of us awkwardly craning our necks to reach. Although it's quick, it's somehow more meaningful than all the making out we already did this morning.

Maybe because it's out in the open rather than in the privacy of his flat. There's not a soul around, but I still feel like we've announced our love to the world. It's nice. Freeing.

"So, what's in the bags?" I ask finally.

Sean sits up straight with a crooked grin on his face. "You'll see."

I lean back with one of my arms propping me up and watch him while he unpacks a selection of fancy little boxes, as well as a bottle of champagne and two glasses.

He needn't have done this, not on his day off. But I'm glad that he did. That means he's all in, doesn't it? We're exactly where we're supposed to be today.

He uncorks the bottle and pours me some. I almost protest that I'm driving, but one glass shouldn't harm anything. I wait while he pours his own and raises it in my direction.

"To us." We clink our glasses together.

"I love you," I blurt out, then bite my bottom lip while staring at him to gauge his reaction.

He doesn't break eye contact even for a second. My heart is racing. We've known each other for just over a week. It's way too soon for any of this, isn't it? Even if I felt this way from the moment we first woke up next to each other. I've fallen hard and I've fallen quickly.

"Lily…" he whispers.

"You don't have to," I tell him, smiling briefly. Stupid me and my stupid big mouth.

"Lily, I have some things to tell you."

"Anything." I press my lips together and wait, holding my breath. I feel like my heartbeat is so loud, it can be heard over the rolling waves lapping at the coastline all around us.

He takes a sip from his glass and briefly averts his gaze. There's a flutter in his lips, like he's not sure whether to smile or what. Or how to begin. Then, he trains his eyes on me again.

"I've been married twice before."

I nod. I knew that already. Along with everyone who watched that video clip I found on YouTube yesterday, plus whoever tuned in to the original broadcast on TV.

"The first time, we were very young. Too young to know what we were doing. My career had just begun. It lasted all of six months before we called it quits."

Everything that came before, it's fine. I won't hold any part of his past against him, as long as he's mine. But all I manage to say is just: "It's okay."

He nods slowly, then carries on talking. "The

second time, with Susan. That was something else. Nine years we tried. We fought like cats and dogs. That flat…"

"The flat." I nod. That's what that video clip was about.

"It was my last attempt at changing things around. I knew she wasn't happy. I wasn't ever there for her. I was too focused on my work. And too arrogant to do anything beyond trying to buy her favor. I'd be on the road doing shows, not coming home for weeks. Then when I finally had a little time, I didn't know how to just *be*, you know? I was so used to always being on the move."

I nod again. Yeah, that sounds a bit like Sean alright.

"Then there was the drinking, the other stuff. I was a handful. Never happy. Never satisfied. I can't blame her for checking out of the marriage when she did."

I put my hand on his arm. Whatever he's telling me, I can feel there's so much other stuff still left unsaid. He's taking the blame for how things ended back then, which is admirable. But he's also putting on a tough front, which I can see right through. It takes two to tango. The clip I saw yesterday broke my heart, because no matter how tough he tried to appear, I could *feel* how broken up he was. And the story he told himself about it all was that he's unlovable. He's wrong, but it sure explains a lot.

"You've changed, though," I remark, squeezing his arm.

"Have I?" There's a skeptical look in his eye.

"You're here with me today, enjoying a well-deserved day off. And until a second ago, you looked pretty satisfied and present in the moment to me."

He grins briefly. "I suppose, yeah. I just…"

"It's fine, really. Everyone has baggage."

Sean scoffs. "Some of us just have a couple of decades more of it."

I shrug. "At least you're not homeless and on job seeker's benefits. Unlike some of us," I tease. Only a part of me is joking.

"A temporary setback. And as long as I'm around, you'll never be homeless."

I can feel myself blushing. A rare feat, which Sean manages to achieve time and time again.

He hooks his arm around my neck and kisses me again, this time harder and deeper than before. The gesture reminds me of our first kiss, even though I initiated that one back at the White Hart. He pulls away a little while later and looks me in the eye again like only he can.

"I wanted to tell you about my history, because I care a great deal about you," he says.

He didn't quite say the L-word, but it's good enough to create a lump in my throat. I bite my lip and smile.

"Okay, well, we'd better start eating before a bunch of renegade seagulls steal all our food," I remark.

He chuckles and shakes his head.

"I'm not kidding, there's one right there!" I gesture at one such feathered thief, which is already gleefully eyeing us and our supplies from about ten feet away.

I hand Sean a plate and cutlery, while he opens the first of the dainty little boxes he carried along and carefully places a French pastry onto my plate. Despite the thumb print he leaves on its side, it's still almost too pretty to eat.

"These look amazing!" I say.

He smiles and opens another box, revealing yet another little culinary work of art.

This is a far cry from the supermarket stuff I grew up eating… as well as everything else I've packed for today.

"Open wide," he tells me, scooping up some of it with his spoon.

It tastes even better than it looks. Like a sweet, fruity cloud with just a hint of vanilla and something else I can't put my finger on.

The sandwiches, somewhat crooked sausage rolls, and slightly over baked lemon drizzle cake I'd prepared for today are no patch on Sean's contribution to our picnic.

"You made all this?" He points at the rather basic fare I plate up in front of him.

I nod shyly.

"You *have* been practicing!"

"They're just sandwiches and stuff," I mumble. "No biggie."

He shakes his head and smiles. "Best picnic I've ever had."

As I watch him enthusiastically taste a little bit of everything I've prepared, I realize that he's right. The food doesn't really matter right now, the company does. This truly is the best picnic ever. Sean's Awesome Day Off is everything I could have hoped for and more.

CHAPTER THIRTEEN

*** Sean ***

It starts like every other day this week. Just another episode, featuring some regular panelists, as well as some fresh-faced younger comedians.

I don't notice the slightly different vibe in the studio, at least not at first. Nor the whispers from the audience and knowing glances from my colleagues. All of it should have tipped me off, but I started the day with my rose-tinted glasses firmly on. It has been like this ever since Lily came into my life and more so after the wonderful day we had yesterday.

She's all I've been able to think about.

We confessed our feelings to each other—well, sort of. She told me she loved me. It was crazy. I couldn't quite bring myself to use those same words, even if I know they're true. I've known it since that first morning I woke up in her company. But 'love' is such an overused word nowadays. I'm not sure it accurately describes the depth and breadth of what I feel for her. That's why I told her about my past. She deserves to know everything, who I really am.

But that was yesterday. Today is another day. Today I'm back at work, and Lily is at home, no doubt applying for more jobs. It's adorable how much she's been worrying about that. It's only been a couple of weeks since she seriously started to look. In the grand scheme of things, that's nothing.

When my phone buzzes in between takes, it automatically makes me smile. But it's not Lily like I was expecting; instead the short message I find is from Ian, my manager. He asks if there's ' *something going on which he should know about*' and a link to some gossip website I really don't want to open. He knows better than to contact me with rumors, especially during shooting hours, so I have to assume there's a valid reason for the interruption. Whatever he sent me, I already know it's going to be bad news.

Still, I resist the urge to check until after we wrap up for the day, because it will surely throw me off my game. I find a quiet corner backstage after the shoot and check my phone again. There's already a lump growing in my throat, and my heart has started to race, because I know exactly where this is going.

The pictures above the fold are innocuous for the most part: Lily and I at the beach. Sharing a kiss in the car. Holding hands while we walk. Lounging on the picnic blanket and feeding each other. Just like a regular couple. Even though the photographer must have been quite far off, and as such, the photos are blurry, her beautiful smile is clear as day in every single one of them. As is her gorgeous youthful figure, which stands in stark contrast to my middle-aged dad bod.

The write-up could wipe the smile off anyone's face, though.

"Nothing to offer women, except money? Comedian-past-his-prime Sean Cleary's seaside outing with a girl half his age. Gold digger? Future ex-wife? Read on and find out!"

I groan. They just *had* to, didn't they? Quoting my own material to me, no less. Some filthy scumbag decided to follow us, hide in the bushes at the beach, and ruin the only perfect thing I've ever had in my entire life. For what? Cheap entertainment for the plebs and a pay day for him.

I don't want to read on. What I really want is to close the site and forget I ever saw it, but my eyes are drawn to the portrait shot of Lily further down the page… She's wearing a fucking school uniform! The picture is obviously from a good number of years ago, but it's damning anyway. They went straight for maximum impact by playing up the age gap angle. How did they even dig that up so quickly?

This was exactly the sort of thing I was worried about. I should have listened to my instincts and not agreed to that outing in the first place. I should have known better than to put both of us in this situation! If only we'd stayed home, she could have been spared this ordeal.

This was always going to happen, you idiot! The little voice in my head chides me. *She's a human being, not a coin collection; can't lock her away forever!*

Hard as I try to keep calm, I'm furious. Confused. Filled with a blind panic so strong, I don't even acknowledge anyone on my way out. They'll understand. Or not. I don't care.

I rush to my car, which is already waiting outside, and instruct Fred to put his foot down. I have to see her right-fucking-now. I have to do some damage control. I have to—

The brief moment of eye contact with Fred in the rear-view as I get in tells me he already knows. Of course he does. He always knows everything. He also knows better than to try and talk to me when I'm like this.

On the way out of the studio gates, I can see the vultures already circling. Paparazzi with their giant cameras, hoping to catch a candid shot of me at my worst. Again.

I lean back in my seat and try to breathe. My windows are tinted, so there's little chance of anyone getting a decent photo. That's not even what I'm worried about right now. I'm one bad decision away from going out there and breaking some stuff. Wouldn't be the first time. I resist the urge with great difficulty.

Capable as always, Fred smoothly pulls away into traffic. After following a few shortcuts only he knows about, he reaches St. James's Park in record time. We don't speak a word during the entire drive.

I mess up twice, punching the wrong code into the security system at the front door. And then, the lift takes an absolute age to get me to the correct floor. I'm out of breath with panic by the time I reach the door and am hit with a feeling of dread so strong, I barely want to turn the key…

What awaits me inside is even worse than I could have predicted.

I'd wanted to get here ahead of time. I wanted to be the one—

Lily is sitting cross-legged on the living room carpet, surrounded by papers and magazines. Every single one is carrying the same story with the same photos of us, even if the headlines are slightly different. The underlying message is all the same.

I should have known. This sort of shit spreads like wildfire.

She looks up, and I can see that her eyes are puffy and streaks of mascara stain her cheeks.

"Sean, I'm so sorry!" She doesn't even finish that sentence before bursting into tears and covering her face with her hands.

My baby. My angel. Why did they have to do this to her? What has this beautiful soul ever done to anyone? She doesn't deserve to be treated like this!

I take a couple of steps to bridge the gap between us and sink down onto my knees beside her, before wrapping my arms around her. Her little body shudders in my embrace. Then, she presses her face into my chest and clings onto me for dear life.

"Why would they write all this? Why would they do this?" she sobs. "It's not even true! I'm not with you for your money!"

"I know, baby. They don't deal in truth, they—" My voice breaks, and I realize I'm crying too.

This is horrific. My entire justification for us being together—for Lily and I becoming a couple—was that I'd do my best to take care of her. That I'd keep her safe. What an absolute failure I am.

Ever since meeting her, her wellbeing and happiness had become my main life goal. My one mission. And I've failed so miserably at that, I'm not sure where to go from here. What kind of a man lets his woman down like this? Not much of a man, I conclude.

I should have known. Instead, I let this fantasy we've lived together since our first meeting convince me that we had a shot. But guys like me don't get that many chances. Mine have been well and truly used up. You could fill a small library with bad press about me from over the years. Of course they jumped at the chance to stab the knife in deeper. What the hell was

I thinking?

"Sean, what do we do? How do we fix this?" she asks.

That breaks me all over again. There's no fixing this. There's just lying down and taking the beating until they move on to something else.

"Sweetheart, we can't," I mumble. "I'm sorry."

"Well, can't we do some kind of tell-all interview? Clear things up?"

I shake my head. Instead of answering her, I just keep caressing her hair and holding her tight. She doesn't know. She doesn't know the level of evil we're dealing with. There's no reasoning with these people! They're not interested in the truth, they just want a good story to sell more copies of their venom-filled magazines! It doesn't matter to them who they hurt in the process.

And the worst part is: they'll keep doing it. As long as it sells more papers, or advertising space, they'll flog the same dead horse, over and over and over again.

As long as we're together, she'll be a target too.

Shit. I've made her a target…

"The best we can hope for is for all this to blow over," I tell her, my voice raspy with emotion. "If we draw more attention to ourselves, the story will never die."

"How did they even manage to follow us?" Lily

complains.

That question crossed my mind too. And the most obvious answer to it only deepens my guilt. The little trip to the bakery I made that morning, picking up pastries to enjoy on our day trip… It was *me* who brought this on the two of us. In my excitement to do a little something in return for her planning something nice for my day off, I forgot to act discreet.

When does a single, middle-aged D-list celebrity ever walk into a fancy French bakery to buy an ungodly amount of dessert and a bottle of expensive champagne just for himself? And that too, with a dumb post-coital grin on his face. That's right, never. I might as well have walked around the neighborhood with a megaphone, announcing our budding relationship to the world. Obviously, word got around, and someone followed us from then on…

The fact is the magic little bubble we've been living in for the past week or so has been destroyed forever. And now there's no putting it back together. From now, there are always going to be a few people hiding in the bushes whenever we leave the house.

She'll never be protected from the spotlight. Not as long as she's here with me.

And I can't do a damn thing about it. I can't call the police on everyone who decides to sit on the nearest park bench for the foreseeable future, can I?

I can't protect her anymore.

No, it's time we face reality. The honeymoon is over and reality has reared its ugly head. Beautiful as our time together was, it has to end now. For her sake.

What is done is done. At least they didn't get anything more revealing than Lily in beach wear. She can still come back from this. She's young. She can simply move on and live a happy life with some much more deserving guy, far away from the all-seeing lenses of the tabloid press.

Far away from me.

"Sean…" Lily sniffles.

I can't even look her in the eye anymore, so I just shake my head. "I'm so sorry you had to deal with this."

"What do you mean 'had to', like past tense?" she asks.

I press my lips together and try to take a deep breath to pull myself together, but the tears are still flowing. I'd be embarrassed about it, if I wasn't so preoccupied with trying to find the right words to say what needs to be said.

"Sean, what are you—" Lily never finishes her question, just stares at me with those same wide green eyes that have continued to captivate me all week.

"I'm sure there are at least half a dozen camera lenses pointed at the windows and the front door by now."

"Your other place, then?" she mumbles.

"They definitely have that address already."

"But…"

"I want to make it very clear that you are welcome to stay here as long as you like. I promised to help you out and I'm a man of my word. But—"

"You won't stay with me anymore." Lily sounds choked.

"I can't, Lily. I can't be responsible for—"

She shakes me off and wraps her arms around herself instead. She looks so small and fragile right now. If my heart wasn't already shattered, this sight would have done it all over again.

"Yesterday…" Lily says, while staring at the ground. "I thought…"

"Sweetheart, don't you see? You'll be fine. It's a matter of a couple of weeks, and they'll move on to someone else."

"Will you?" she snaps. "Will you move on to someone else?"

I finally meet her gaze for the first time since all of this began. The intensity in her stare gives me chills.

"Never."

I can't imagine ever putting anyone else in this position ever again. I'll never forget her. Never stop loving her. I'll have to comfort myself with the knowledge that for once in my life I actually thought about someone other than myself. That in letting her go, I am setting her free.

She'll go on to live her life. Have a family. Find happiness.

I'll focus on my work. It's all I'm good for. My relationships are all doomed to fail anyway.

As hard as this is, I know it's for the best.

*** Lily ***

I still can't believe what happened. It's been an hour or so since Sean packed up his things and left, and I've done nothing except stare at the walls in between bouts of further tears.

My entire body and most of all my head aches like crazy. But my heart just feels numb, and that's possibly what hurts the most.

Just twenty-four hours ago, I had everything I could ever ask for. After the high that was yesterday's perfect day with Sean, everything came crumbling down on top of me today.

Why did this have to happen? Why did some asshole photographer have to see us and ruin everything we had? Sean even started to open up to me, just like I'd hoped. A few hours alone at the beach made us grow closer as a couple than all the sex we'd had this past week. Except, perhaps it didn't. It was all an illusion. And today, the magic is gone.

The write-up that accompanied the photos didn't come as much of a surprise to me. Everything they said was stuff I'd already considered. All my worst fears, laid out for the world to read. That I'm a gold digger who would have never looked twice at him if not for his money. That I'm never going to amount to anything, that I have no prospects and so I'm looking for a handout…

I tried to tell him it's not true. I've tried to tell him—and more importantly, show him—from the day we met that I wanted to be with him no matter who he is. But in the face of the overwhelming evidence, printed in black and white for everyone to see, what is he to believe? I can't even blame him, because I've always been painfully aware of how bad things look between us.

That's why he didn't tell me he loved me yesterday. He still had his reservations, deep down.

Before he left, he told me I could stay here as long as I like. Thinking about the expression on his face when he said it makes the tears start up again. What I saw in his eyes wasn't malicious intent or anger; it was pain. He looked so hurt. And I couldn't do a damn thing about it. Even my best efforts weren't good enough to convince him of my motives. By the time I realized what he was telling me, he'd already made up his mind, so I didn't even try.

I try to swallow my sorrow. Because my head just can't take it anymore. It's splitting in half with the beginnings of a migraine. If I cry any more, it's bound to explode.

I decide to have a shower. A long, hot shower, to

wash all the dirt away.

By the end of it, I'm bright red and empty, with nothing more left to give.

This thing we had, it was always too good to be true. I should have trusted my instincts and realized I'm just not relationship material. And especially not for a guy like Sean. I'm a bit of fun. A toy. A fleeting fascination, destined to go through loser boyfriends like Mom, but never truly settling down. Because who will have me once they realize there's not much substance beyond the pretty exterior?

I don't know how to be a partner. Or a wife. I'm not responsible like Alexis. I thought I could learn with Sean, but... This chance has been taken away from me. This is just the latest in the long list of failed relationships that came before. I've never had an issue attracting a man's attention. But keeping it, that's a whole other story.

And the tears start back up again, no matter how hard I try to force them down.

I'm so exhausted I lie down on the bed, staining my pillow with my wet hair. But there's no rest to be found here. Not with Sean's scent clinging to the sheets and memories of us etched in my mind.

I'm sure that's why he left so quickly. Because being here was just too painful.

It's too painful for me as well. And so, after catching my breath for a few more minutes, I also decide to pack up, just to have something to do. It's too late to try and go anywhere, so I'll be leaving first thing in the morning instead.

I'm still brooding when the sound of my phone startles me. For a split second, I hope it's Sean, but I check my expectations before even looking at the screen.

It's not going to be Sean. I'm never going to hear from him again.

Instead, it's Alexis. I cut the call. I'll just blubber uncontrollably if I try to speak, so what's the point?

She calls back immediately. When I cut that too, she sends me a message.

'Talk to me, dammit! I'm worried about you.'

I stare at it for a moment, but my emotions start to overflow again when I type my response.

'Sean and I broke up.'

Through my tears, I can see her type and stop typing a couple of times. Finally, her reply comes through.

'Text me the address. I'm coming over.'

I make a face and shake my head. I really don't want to see her right now. But the prospect of spending the night alone is much, much worse. Still, I remember what Sean said about this place being watched by the press. And the last thing anyone needs is for Alexis to get dragged into this mess as well.

'No. I'll come to you. Working tonight?' I write.

'Yes, but I'll leave right now and wait for you at home.'

I take a few deep breaths to calm myself.

"Okay," I say. "Okay, let's do this."

My stuff is already mostly packed in the same collection of mismatched luggage I arrived here with just over a week ago. By the time the Uber gets here, I'll tidy up the rest. A part of me is glad Alexis reached out. The less time I have to spend in this place now that everything's gone to shit, the better.

Unfortunately, that feeling doesn't last long. When I reach her place thirty minutes later, and see that half of her stuff has been packed up in boxes, I finally understand why she was being so abrasive when I asked to crash on her couch for a while. She's moving in with Bob now that she's expecting. It makes sense. But I'm disappointed she didn't just come out and tell me that.

I guess everyone is moving on to better things. Everyone but me; I seem to be going backwards at an alarming pace.

We don't talk much all night. Mainly because every time she tries to, it comes out so judgmental and angry that I shut her down. Annoying boyfriend or not, maybe it wouldn't be so bad to just head to Mom's house come morning.

***

My first morning back home sets the stage for whatever's yet to come. No matter where I turn, someone wants to lecture me on something. As a result, I spend most of the day locked in my own room, feeling sorry for myself.

When my phone rings late in the afternoon, I feel like smashing it against the wall just in case it's Alexis with a few more nuggets of wisdom. Finally, curiosity gets the better of me and I check the caller ID. It's the last person I would have expected to call me right now.

"Lily! I'm so sorry I didn't call back sooner," Jill says. "Work has been crazy."

"It's okay." I'm not even sure why she's calling right now. When I reached out to her the day I moved out of the flat share, I felt like I was intruding, asking a favor from someone I used to know a long time ago. Then again, I never actually asked for that favor, so she'd have no idea why I was reaching out.

"How are you holding up? I—umm—saw the papers, obviously."

I shrug. Not that she can see. "This too shall pass."

"I know we haven't been in regular touch for a couple of years, but we're still friends, right? You can talk to me."

I frown and press my lips together. That's sweet of

her, but I'm not sure I want to take the bait. "I don't really feel like talking, though."

"Fair enough. We can just listen to each other breathe," she remarks.

That makes me chuckle a little. "I mean… What's there to say that the tabloids haven't already printed?"

"I'd like to think I know you, Lily. All that stuff is a load of shit."

I scoff. I wish Sean had realized that too.

"I feel like for a moment there, I was somebody. The way he looked at me, like… Damn. I'm not making any sense, am I?" I say.

"What do you mean 'was'?" she asks.

"Oh, they haven't printed that bit yet, have they? It's over."

"Sheesh. That sucks."

"Yeah. It was nice while it lasted," I say. "Now I've come slinking back home to my childhood bedroom to listen to Mom lecture me on how to keep a man." I turn onto my side and stare at the faded poster on the wall that harks back to my awkward girl band phase in high school.

"Oh man. Your mom doesn't mince her words, does she?"

I click my tongue. "She's the expert, you know."

"Right."

There's an awkward silence between us. Finally, Jill gets the hidden meaning in my words and starts to giggle. "You're terrible!"

"So I've read," I say.

Our exchange makes me smile despite myself. We might have grown apart ever since Jill went to college, but she's one of the very few people who still gets me, it seems.

"How come you're back home? Last I heard you'd scored some cushy desk job? Does the corporate world pay that badly?" Jill asks.

I sigh and shake my head. "I got laid off. That was the whole reason I went to Alexis' work that night when I first met Sean. I told you she works in a pub now, right?"

"Right."

"Anyway, so that's how all of this started..." Another deep breath later, and somehow I end up telling Jill the whole story, beginning to end. Minus the X-rated bits. Although I'd been adamant with everyone else that I don't really want to talk about it, it still feels like a relief to finally let it all out.

"Sounds like a fairytale, except, you know..." Jill says.

"More like one of those original uncensored Grimm's ones, where everyone dies at the end."

She doesn't laugh. There's just eerie silence on the other end of the line.

"Lily, don't take this the wrong way, but I'm going to have to call you back."

I sigh and close my eyes. I guess this is the wrong way to rekindle an old friendship—by unloading all your emotional bullshit onto them the second they call to catch up.

"Okay, Jill. I'm sorry for being such a downer."

"Don't even, Lily! I'll call you right back, I promise!"

I shrug and put the phone down before turning onto my back and staring at the ceiling. The glow-in-the-dark stickers I'd stuck all over the ceiling when I was thirteen have started to yellow and peel over the years. I wonder if they'll still light up.

I doubt Jill is going to call. I wouldn't call me back right now.

But, true to her word, the phone does ring again, barely five minutes later.

"Lily, one question."

"Yeah?"

"You need a job pretty badly, right?" she asks.

"If I ever want to move out of my childhood bedroom again, yeah."

"It's entry level—technically an internship, but with pay—and it's just a short-term contract, but if you like the work and do your best, you'll probably get another project soon after, so I hope you don't mind—"

"I'll take anything," I interrupt her. Literally anything at this point. I've only just arrived back in this house, but I've got to get out of here before I lose my mind.

"Awesome! Here's the deal." Jill starts to tell me all about her current job. About how she's second-in-command on the production team of a reality TV dating show called *Sealed with a Kiss*, and her assistant has just quit due to health reasons. Apparently, they're urgently looking for someone to take over, because they're in the middle of shooting the first season.

The details are a bit fuzzy, but I suppose they don't really matter. Jill has offered me a job, and I'm going to take it. Anything to get out of here as soon as possible!

CHAPTER FIFTEEN

*** Sean ***

Go to work, get through my lines, come home, drink too much, go to sleep. Or should I say pass out? Rinse and repeat.

It's been a week since I last saw Lily. A week of pure agony, dulled only by the insane amount of alcohol I've been drinking, and the thought that despite everything, I still have her best interests at heart. Fuck me, it wasn't easy, but it had to be done.

After the absolute creaming she got in the national tabloid press, with every second gossip rag in the country combing through her past to try and find any little thing to smear her with, it was the least I could do for her. I had to let her go before this thing between us crushed her spirit forever.

Being in the spotlight is never easy. And it certainly isn't something everyone can or should deal with. I chose it for myself, when I pursued my comedy career. But she didn't. And so she shouldn't have to put up with it on my account.

Whatever has been written is already out there forever, but the constant churn of the news cycle ensures that most of the country will have forgotten all about Lily by next week.

I won't, though. I'll never forget her. I'll never get over this loss. She was the second chance—third chance, technically—in life which I never deserved. She was the *one*.

She's young enough to get another chance for herself. I hope that she will find happiness one day soon, with a man who deserves her, because I don't and I won't. It's probably for the best too, because everything I touch inevitably turns to shit. That's what happened with my marriage with Susan, and Alison before her. Hell, even my brother Jack could tell I'm a fuck-up back when we were just kids. And that's what happened with Lily too, only much faster and more intense. I knew she'd be the end of me the moment I first saw her. I'm almost there. Almost at rock bottom.

I'm in the car on the way home. My *real* home. Not the make-believe home I'd shared with Lily for all of one week. I'm not sure what day it is, except that it's a weekday, probably. Details like these don't seem to matter anymore.

My phone buzzes, making me flinch. Sleep deprivation is putting me on edge. I haven't been checking my messages, so I'm about to ignore it again, but this time it's a call, so the damn thing keeps on buzzing and buzzing. It's getting on my nerves.

"Yeah," I answer, clearing my throat.

"Sean. I've been trying to track you down for days. Where have you been?" Ian sounds irate. I suppose he has reason to be, but I'm not in the right frame of mind to be questioned.

"Been busy. You know how it is; we're mid-season. What's going on?"

"Right, so the network wants to start teasing the upcoming show on social media. Have you got a title for it yet?"

I pinch the bridge of my nose. Upcoming special. *Fuck!* What's the date today?

"Is it too late to cancel that?" I ask.

The line goes silent for a moment. I can just imagine the face on him while he melts down completely.

"I'm going to pretend I didn't hear that, Sean." There's an icy quality in Ian's voice which I know to mean he's pissed. Seething, even.

"Fine. I'm only joking," I grumble. "Remember jokes?"

"What is it this time? Don't tell me you're using again! I doubt the network would take kindly to another scandal like that!" Ian threatens.

I take a deep breath and shake my head. "I'm not doing that shit anymore."

"It's about the girl then, isn't it? Hang tight, they're going to get bored with the story any day now."

"Yeah, I know." *They* might get bored. But I'll still

be hurting once it's all over. This is one wound that will never heal.

"Well then, I need to give them *something* by day-after at the latest. You always say you work best under pressure. The pressure is bloody well on now!"

"Relax. I won't let you down," I mumble.

"You'd be letting yourself down more," Ian says.

I shake my head. Who does he think he is, my old man? Nah, knowing the hateful bastard that he was, he wouldn't have wasted words on me but let his belt do the talking instead.

The line goes silent and I sit there, stunned, for a moment. He's right about one thing. The pressure is most definitely on. Rather than head home where I'll inevitably end up drowning my sorrows in some overpriced Scotch, I figure I have to make a change. Get back into a productive routine of some sort. It's no use to anyone—least of all me—if I burn my bridges with the network that's keeping the lights on in my house.

"Fred, turn it around. Let's go to the White Hart," I say.

"Very good, sir," Fred responds. Considering that's the most he's said to me over the last couple of days of driving me to and from the studio, I'll have to assume that he approves of my decision. I glance up at his face in the rear-view. He looks thoughtful and stoic like he always does.

"Thanks, Fred," I say.

He nods at me, then trains his eyes on the road again as he turns into a narrow alleyway away from the main road. One of his many secret shortcuts, no doubt.

I turn and look out the window at the abandoned-looking offices and parking garages passing me by, while trying to brainstorm. My head still aches, just like it has done every single day since... Since Lily. I force my thoughts away from her and back on task.

The special is supposed to be forty-five minutes long. How am I going to write enough material to fill that time, when I feel like I have nothing left to give? It's a miracle I've been able to do my job every day— mostly because there's a room full of young comedic writers taking care of my monologues. And I've been getting through any improv routines by being a miserable git, roasting absolutely anyone and anything I can get a cheap laugh out of. At least the audience has been enjoying it.

Guess that's the answer. The worse I feel and the more cynical and caustic I become, the more laughs I get. Throughout the remainder of the drive to Teddington, I try to figure out exactly how much of my current heartache I'll be willing to share to salvage my career. As Fred pulls into the narrow driveway leading to the back of the pub, I think I've got my answer.

Everything. I'm going to go all out. Balls to the wall. Otherwise, I'll have nothing.

Fred goes in first to make sure my route is clear, and to quietly tell Alexis and Bob that I've arrived. Two minutes later, I follow and take a seat in that same old room.

On that same creaky chair, at the same spot at the well-worn wooden table. My spot. My seat. I don't feel quite right being here, but what choice do I have?

Alexis greets me with a glare while she silently serves me my drink. I suppose her frosty welcome is well deserved. I'm relieved when she leaves without saying a word.

A few moments later, the door opens again. This time it's Bob.

"Mate." He approaches my seat and greets me with a pat on the back. "Mind if I join you for a second?"

I shrug and turn part of the way to face him. That's when I notice that the door is still partially open, and Alexis is waiting with her hands folded across her chest. Yeah, I definitely feel unwelcome. But I can't muster the energy to care about what anyone thinks about me. The only person I still care about is no longer a part of my life.

"How's it going, Bob?" I mumble.

"It's fine. Been a couple of weeks since you last came in. How are *you* doing?" Bob asks.

I take a big sip and close my eyes. They burn. My throat burns. My head throbs. I don't know why he always wants to talk. What's there to say?

"Oh, you know. Been better." I put the glass back down and stare at the droplets of condensation that have formed on the outside of it. Maybe I shouldn't be here after all. The place where everything began. It might have turned into my preferred writing spot once Bob took over the pub, but all the events of the past couple of weeks are still too fresh in my memory to ignore. Plus, there's Alexis, who looks in a good mood to give me a well deserved bollocking.

"This was a bad idea," I grumble, pushing my chair back.

"Wait a minute." Bob puts his hand on my shoulder. "You only just got here."

I glance back at the half-open door. My preferred escape route. Alexis is still blocking it.

Bob leans back in his chair. "I know you're hurting, old friend. But there's nothing heroic in going through it alone. You were there for me during my divorce. The least I can do is offer a sympathetic ear now."

I scoff. "I really don't want to talk about it. I'm only here because I really need to get some writing done, or else I'll ruin my career on top of everything else. I don't much care at this point, but Ian made it pretty clear he wants his cut from the upcoming show, so…"

Bob turns. "Can you get us another round, please, dear?"

I rest my head on my left hand, still holding on to the half-empty glass with my right.

"She's pissed, isn't she? I'm sorry." I sigh.

"Don't worry about that. How are you holding up?" Bob asks.

I scoff. "About as well as you'd think. Seriously. When—*if*—I want to talk, I'll call you."

"Okay. We can just sit. Have a drink."

Footsteps approach from behind. Quick, angry footsteps. Alexis puts two full glasses in front of us just a little bit too hard, causing some of their contents to slosh over the edge and onto the table.

"Okay. He's your best friend, and I respect that. But she's my *cousin,* dammit! So, please forgive me for butting in here, but I think I have the right to say a few words!"

"I really don't think this is the right time, dear," Bob pleads.

I close my eyes and shake my head. "Let her talk."

She takes a deep breath. Funny, how something as innocuous a simple inhale can sound angry, coming from Alexis. "Look at me, Sean."

I make a face.

"Be nice," Bob whispers.

"It's okay. Really," I mumble as I look up at her,

looming over me with a dangerous scowl on her face. The last thing I want on my conscience is to be the reason for a falling out between these two. Yet another relationship to turn to shit because of me. No, thank you!

"Okay. Here goes. I mean this in the nicest possible way, but you, Sean, are being an absolute wanker!"

Bob clears his throat, but knows better than to stand in her way now that she's starting to let loose.

"I can't begin to explain how sorry I am about everything. I never meant for Lily to get hurt," I say.

She rolls her eyes. "Lily can be stupidly impulsive, incredibly irresponsible, and infuriatingly dumb in a lot of ways. But she's the absolute kindest soul I've ever seen."

I nod. "Yep." And that's why I couldn't stand what happened to her.

"She's the most loving person, even when people treat her like shit, which might I say has been a common theme throughout her life. She's sensitive, maybe even a little naive. Loyal to a fault," Alexis continues.

I nod again. All of the above.

"And you threw her away, for what? Some dumb headlines nobody even cares about?"

I frown. "No! What?"

"She would have stood with you until the very

end—God knows why, honestly—but she would have. And you just cut her loose as soon as things get a little difficult? What the fuck does that make you? You're even worse than her dad, who left her before she was even born!" Alexis rants.

Her words hurt deeply, which is quite a feat, because I thought I'd achieved maximum heartache already a week ago when I walked out of the flat at St. James's Park and with it, out of Lily's life. I try to breathe steadily, but she's still managed to knock the wind out of me. I have no words.

Bob puts his hand on her arm. "I think that's quite enough, dear."

She shakes him off. "I'll decide when it's enough, thank-you-very-much."

Their short exchange allows me to formulate the beginnings of a response. "I needed to protect her from—"

"*Protect* her? How does breaking her heart achieve that exactly?" Alexis demands.

"She'll be better off. She can still have a life. Find happiness—"

"Sean. Just fucking stop!"

I look up at her again.

"She *was* happy! I'd never seen her as happy as when she told me you two were an item, and every day since! I don't think this is about *her* or her happiness at all. You want to know what I think,

Sean?" she rages on.

She juts out her chin in my direction, as if to challenge me. I'm way too numb to let her rile me up any further, so I just sigh and wait, with my head in my hands, for her to complete her lecture. Lily wasn't wrong when she said Alexis was a hard-ass.

"I think you're scared. You're so fucking scared of being happy yourself, that's why you pulled the plug at the first sign of trouble. This entire thing has nothing to do with Lily at all!"

I raise my head again and stare at her blankly for a few seconds.

Bob takes her hand and squeezes it briefly.

"I'm almost done!" Alexis tells him, then trains her eyes on me again. "Sean. I hope you're hearing me."

"I was trying to keep her safe." I sigh. "I didn't want her to have to live her life in the spotlight, and deal with all the judgments and trolling… I signed up for it, knowing the risks. She didn't. When I came home to her reading all that filth… You should have seen her. I couldn't put her in that situation again."

She scoffs. "You have no clue, do you? She's been calling me every damn night since it happened. And you know what she talks about?"

I shake my head.

"She asks if *you* came in at all. How *you're* doing. She cries on the phone every time she spots a new article about the two of you, not because she gives two shits about what they write about her, but because she thinks you believed what they wrote. And how all that stuff affects *you*."

I groan. I'm about one deep breath away from breaking down myself. She thinks I believe all those filthy lies? What the hell?

"Yeah! I tried telling her she doesn't need a coward like you in her life, but she couldn't care less what I think either. All she cares about is *Sean, this; Sean, that.* Like, what the fuck else did you want out of a relationship? Unless you were just playing her."

"I would never!" I protest.

"Then think long and hard about what you've done. It's all I can ask. For both your sakes, but mainly hers." She huffs angrily. "Okay. *Now* I'm done."

Alexis steps away from the table and leaves Bob and me without looking back even once.

"Ooookay," Bob says, taking a big sip from his glass and shaking his head.

I follow his example, still overwhelmed with everything Alexis piled on top of me just now. She's certainly not one to mince her words. But does that make her wrong?

"I'm going to need some time. Alone." My voice sounds more choked than expected.

Bob nods, picks up his glass, and leaves me as well. The silence the two of them leave behind is deafening.

Minute after minute passes while I try to collect my thoughts, but they're too jumbled to make sense of. In the end, I take out my phone, open the voice recorder app, and just start to unload into it. I'll untangle all of it later, maybe. But for now, it's the only way I know how to make it stop hurting so damn much. I don't want a sympathetic ear or a shoulder to cry on. I don't want feedback or analyses. It's like a pressure release valve has been opened, and I can't help but keep going until I have nothing left to give.

CHAPTER SIXTEEN

* Lily *

It's been four weeks. Four weeks and counting from the day I moved out of Sean's flat and back in with Mom and her douchebag boyfriend. I refuse to remember his name, because he's not going to stick around. They never do…

Sean told me I could stay at his place as long as I wanted to, because that's just the kind of guy he is. Kind hearted and generous, despite everything that went down since our beach outing together.

But I couldn't. I couldn't spend another minute there, being reminded of everything we had and everything I'd lost. And instinctively, I understood that my presence there would only hurt him too.

I understand why he called it quits, deep down I do. I'm no prize. A naive little girl with no prospects and seemingly no ambitions beyond snagging herself a famous guy as a sugar daddy. I might look nice in a bikini (thanks, sleazy photographer who followed us to the beach) or spread out naked on a king-sized bed. But I'm not the sort of person a sensible, mature guy like Sean would fantasize about settling down and having a family with. I might make a decent enough fling or even a girlfriend, but I'm not a wife.

Nor am I a mother, like Alexis is going to become in a few months.

It's no wonder he wanted to keep our relationship a secret. And then, the world found out about it anyway and ruined everything before it ever had a chance to develop into something more.

Rationalizing all that doesn't mean that I'm not still shattered, though. I am.

I go through it all every single day, wondering if the gaping hole in my chest will ever heal up again. If I'll ever feel even a fraction of the joy and hope I felt during every moment I shared with Sean.

I have no one to blame but myself, though, as Mom keeps reminding me every chance she gets. Apparently, I should have dressed fancier and pretended to like everything he likes. I shouldn't have been so easy and at least made him buy me nice gifts before sleeping with him. I should have kept staying in the flat for a few months as payment for our time together.

As if that's all it was between us: a transaction.

And Alexis isn't any better, even if she keeps telling me the exact opposite. That he's a useless shit who never deserved me anyway. That I should forget about him and make something of myself, and soon enough, I'll find a good guy who won't drop me at the first sign of trouble like Sean has.

To be honest, I can barely stand being around either of them right now.

Unfortunately, I live with the former now. And the only reason I bear with the latter is because I keep hoping she has news for me. That Sean has come into the White Hart and Alexis can give me some kind of update. That she'll tell me he's doing okay, so at least I'll have one less thing to worry about.

But that hasn't happened. I have no idea how Sean is doing, and it's driving me mad. I'm afraid to turn on the TV and watch any of his live shows, because I don't know what I'll find. Jekyll or Hyde? Or something much, much worse that I haven't seen before?

And what about that comedy special he still had to write? There's been ads in the paper for it, as Mom told me, and tickets are fully sold out. I didn't have the courage to look for it myself, so I took her word for it.

So, I guess the show must go on, as they say. He didn't need a day trip to the beach to find his inspiration and start writing. He just needed to be rid of me.

I was just a distraction, wasn't I? Despite my best efforts, I couldn't leave my roots behind. I was never going to be good enough for a man like him.

Why I ever got my hopes up, I'll never know. Maybe Mom is right. When we're young, we can hook anyone if we play our cards right. But it never lasts. And before you know it, you hit fifty, and your beauty fades and you'll be scraping the bottom of the barrel for losers like *whats-his-name*. Mom's current boyfriend.

God, I'm starting to sound cynical like Alexis, before she got together with Bob and mellowed down some.

The only saving grace in my life right now is the internship Jill arranged for me. She didn't need to, but I'm eternally grateful that she did. Working with her is giving me a purpose. Something else to focus on. It didn't take me long to get settled in and figure out my role. And the rest of the crew have been amazing. It's the sort of supportive atmosphere I'd never encountered at my previous jobs.

The tragedy is that the offer only came along after Sean had already called it quits. A part of me wonders if this new opportunity could have convinced him that I'm not just looking for a handout. That I'm willing to work and make my own way in life and really want *him* instead of just his bank balance.

Unfortunately, I'll never find out the answer to that. It's simply too late.

And right now, it's too late to keep on wallowing at all. I'm due at Claire's office by ten, and the journey takes at least forty minutes by public transport.

So, instead of wasting any more time, I grab my

backpack and head downstairs, where I take a couple of bananas out of the fruit bowl on the dining table as an improvised breakfast and leave without anyone else in the house even noticing. I've found that to be the most bearable approach: just kind of sneak around as if I'm not really here. That way, I don't have to listen to too many lectures or endure forced 'family time' with the boyfriend.

I rush to the bus stop and check the time. With a bit of luck, I'll still make it. I'd hate to come in late when I'm still so new at the job.

The other people waiting don't pay me much attention. Everyone is enjoying the warm late summer weather and minding their own business. Until our double-decker bus finally makes its way around the turn and I let out a very loud gasp at the sight of it, attracting stares all around.

On its side, there's a huge picture of Sean, standing with his arms folded and looking sternly at the camera. The angle at which the photo was taken makes it look like he's staring right at me.

I try, but I just can't look away. I'm just frozen, like a deer in headlights.

The other passengers push past me, mumbling words of disapproval, until I'm the only one left standing on the curb.

"Love, you gonna get on?" The driver snaps his fingers at me to get my attention.

Although my legs feel heavy as lead, I force myself into action and hurriedly touch my card against the scanner as I rush past him. Once inside, everyone has their eyes trained on me already. Like I'm some kind of freak show. On my way to the stairs, an old lady hands me a tissue. That's when I realize I'm crying.

I find an empty seat on the top deck and squeeze up right against the window. I still feel like everyone's looking at me, though.

"Shit," I mutter to myself, trying to make myself even smaller.

I dab my eyes with the tissue, trying not to smudge my eyeliner too much. So much for trying to hold things together all these weeks. Even the forty-minute commute to Hammersmith isn't long enough for me to regain my composure.

As such, I reach the office building with panda eyes and a headache. The only reason I manage to get everyone's drinks order right is because the barista takes pity on me and reminds me what I've been buying every single morning this week.

Jill intercepts me as soon as I arrive.

"I figured you would have seen one of those ads. They're bloody everywhere," she complains.

I sniffle and nod. "It's okay. Can't avoid him forever."

She wraps her arm around me and guides me into the makeshift editing room where Claire and the rest of the team are already hard at work discussing their plans for the day. Discreet as usual, they don't stare or ask awkward questions. Everyone just kind of gets on with their work as normal, allowing me a moment to breathe.

"Lily. Are you okay?" Claire asks when she hands me a checklist of stuff to organize for the next episode we're shooting.

I nod. "Fine."

"Okay." She folds her arms and looks at me for a few seconds. "I haven't spoken to you about this, because the last thing I would want in your position would be to have my boss involved in my personal life, but—"

I shake my head and press my lips together. "It's alright, Claire. I understand."

This is where she tells me she can't keep me on because I've not been focusing on my work. That my attitude is bringing crew morale down. Or whatever. In any case, I'm bracing for impact, and my eyes are prickling already in anticipation for further tears. I feel like this job was my last chance.

"*Sealed with a Kiss* is airing on the same network as Sean Cleary's comedy special," Claire says.

I frown. So? What does that have to do with anything?

"So, if you want, I can arrange a ticket for you to see the recording on Saturday. Maybe clear the air between you two. Whatever."

The shock must be obvious on my face, because Claire smiles briefly before carrying on. "I'm going to take that as a yes. Chin up, Lily. Whatever happens, you're going to land on your feet. I firmly believe that we must stick together and support each other when someone's going through a difficult time. It's why I approved Jill's request to bring you on. Keep an eye on your inbox for that ticket, okay?"

She pats me on the back before leaving me standing there with a mouth full of teeth. A part of me still has no idea what just happened. Do I even want to see his show? I mean… Seeing his picture on the side of a damn bus nearly broke me this morning. What will happen once I see him in person?

Jill joins me a moment later with a look of concern on her face. "What happened? What did Claire want?"

"She…" I take a deep breath and blink a few times. "She's going to get me a ticket to Sean's show."

"Oh!" Jill stares at me with wide eyes. "I thought it was sold out?"

I stare back at her. "I know!"

"Well, do you even want to go?" she asks.

"I have no idea!"

We keep looking at each other in silence, while my heart is racing ever faster.

I'm glad it's Jill I'm talking to about this, and not

Alexis. Because I already know what the latter would think about this. She's been trying to convince me to forget Sean from the moment we broke up. That's not how this stuff works, though. I know I could never leave behind all that we had. Not completely. That one week with Sean has changed me forever.

"It could be emotional," Jill remarks.

I nod. Obviously. "But maybe it'll—I don't know—give me some closure?"

Whatever that means. I'm still thinking about what Claire said about sticking together. That almost makes me cry again. I've never been more grateful for a job which basically consists of fetching coffee, taking notes, and making phone calls. As basic as the work is, the working atmosphere makes all the difference.

Jill nods slowly. "Take your time to decide. And if you want a ride to and from, let me know."

"Thanks, Jill."

She smiles briefly and gives me a half-hug. That's when I finally manage to regain control of myself, take a deep breath, and get to work. We don't have much time before the next episode, and there's a ton of stuff to be done beforehand.

I'll have to consider Claire's offer later, once I get home.

CHAPTER SEVENTEEN

*** Sean ***

I'm always nervous when waiting to go on stage before a live audience. Staring at the black curtains that separate me from the audience, I reflect on everything that's brought me to this point. It's been so many years since my first stand-up gig, but still. That moment of anticipation, that burst of anxiety of 'what if' never fades.

What if the audience doesn't like it?

What if I get bad reviews?

What if nobody laughs and the world finally figures out that I'm a talentless hack?

And today, there's an even bigger question on my mind. What if my set upsets Lily? I'm not expecting her to watch it; not immediately, anyway. But once it airs, the media will eat it up and regurgitate it all over the gossip rags, so the message will reach her loud and clear.

Today is the only way I know how to make a stand. For what I believe in. To let her know how I really feel. She has every right to be angry with me. I don't deserve her forgiveness or another chance at earning it. But I'm fighting for it anyway.

Fighting for her.

Because I love her.

In a few minutes, the entire room of people beyond this curtain will know it. And when the special airs, the whole country. Sooner or later, my message will reach her too. I just can't be sure of how it will be received.

That day at the beach, I didn't tell her, though I felt it so keenly. And I've regretted it ever since. More so after hearing Alexis's well-deserved rant during my last visit to the White Hart. Lily was the best thing to ever happen to me and I fucked it all up.

Maybe I *was* afraid like Alexis said. Afraid of finding happiness as well as of losing it again, once she figured out she could do so much better than me. But what I didn't realize then was that I should have let life take its course. There are no shortcuts, only mistakes.

And this was the biggest one I've ever made. And what I'm about to do is the only thing I could think of to remedy the mess I've made. Though it's probably not going to work.

I can hear the announcer loud and clear beyond the curtain. This is my cue. The moment of truth. I take a deep breath and give myself a last second pep-talk.

Tell the truth. Go all out.

The crowd goes crazy as I walk across the

otherwise empty stage towards the microphone and bar stool that's been set up for me. Although I was tempted to ask for the stagehand to get me a pint of beer to drink during my performance, I've opted for water instead. I'll need to keep my wits about me so I don't mess up again.

As nervous as I was while waiting to go on, I can feel the anxiety fade away now. The stage is a strange place to be. Many hundreds of eyes are on me, fixated on everything I do. But because of the spotlights shining in my face, they're all blurry and indistinguishable. Like they're not real people. And I'm not really here.

But I am. And I'd better act like it.

"Good evening, Hammersmith Apollo!" I call out.

The crowd roars.

"Hope you're all settled in, got yourself a drink, and won't mind if I just dive straight in…" Through the glare of the stage lights, I can see dozens of audience members raise their plastic cups, no doubt to signal that they indeed treated themselves to the overpriced alcoholic beverages from the concessions counter in the lobby.

"There's an elephant in the room today…" I say. "Unless you've been living under a rock this past month, I'm sure you will have read the papers. The many, many papers that had pictures of *this* ugly mug on their front pages." I point at myself with my thumb.

Someone in the back row whoops very loudly. "Yeah, cheers!" I raise my bottle of water in his direction.

"I know you've come to my show today, expecting me to be a good sport and tell a few jokes, and share a few laughs. But I want to get something off my chest first, so I hope you'll bear with me."

I take a deep breath, and try to focus on telling the audience exactly what I've written and rehearsed. For a grand gesture to be effective, it has to be well executed. Otherwise, it'll just come off as desperate and sad.

"For a short while, there was a woman in my life..." I start. "A woman who turned me into a better man. Her name is Lily..."

This is the right thing to do, isn't it? I try to seek out a friendly pair of eyes in the audience to keep me going, but I'm unable to focus on any of them.

So I close my eyes and imagine I'm talking directly to her instead.

"You know I've been alone for a while, ever since my last divorce. It worked fine. I didn't think I was cut out for relationships anyway, so I just got on with things on my own. And then you walked into my life and changed everything."

The audience is quiet. No cheers, no heckles, nothing. It's as if all the people have disappeared and

I'm the last person left in the theater. On stage, I am alone. Just me, myself, and my thoughts. I really wish I'd asked for that beer after all.

"I was selfish; I wanted to keep you to myself. Out of the public eye, away from the spotlight. I thought that if I let anyone get in between, everything would fall apart as things inevitably do…"

I open my eyes again and see the silent crowd before me.

"You've all heard my past material. Hell, you've seen my face in the papers too often after a hard night. I won't lie or dress it up; things have been rough at times. I was a basket case, and I didn't think that could ever really change… Until Lily."

Someone whistles, but is immediately shushed by other audience members. I don't let it distract me from my message.

"I thought I'd come up here tonight to tell the national tabloid press to go fuck itself. For not knowing when to let something be. For inserting themselves into situations they have no means of understanding. For destroying the reputation of an angel." I can feel my voice get louder as I get into the swing of things. This is turning into the rant of all rants. A Sean Cleary special.

"So, I'd like to invite you all to say it with me. Fuck the tabloids!" I wait for a moment to give people the chance to react. There's some careful applause, but that's it. Ah, that's what it feels like to bomb. It's been years, but that feeling is something you'll never forget.

"I've been at this for a while. I know the deal. Who doesn't want to take a few unflattering pictures of a fat, middle-aged man with strong opinions and make fun of him? I'm a big target; I've brought this on myself. But to slander *her*. That's unforgivable. All she ever did was take a liking to a guy who never deserved her. That's punishment in itself, you didn't need to add to it!"

I take a big sip of water, while a wave of reluctant laughter ripples through the audience. Okay, maybe I'm not bombing completely.

"That day was the first time we went anywhere together. I don't take a lot of days off, you know. Always working. Always moving. But she insisted it would be nice. She planned a whole day just for the two of us to spend time together. We talked and we held hands and we did all the dumb stuff teenagers in love do. That's what we were. In love. Though I was too big a chicken shit to tell her when I had the chance, so I'm telling all of you instead. I love her."

I imagine her standing in front of me, melting me with those big, innocent eyes of hers.

"I love you, Lily! Always will. And I don't expect you to forgive me. I don't expect you to endure the bullshit that comes with being in the public eye. The unforgiving and constant scrutiny wouldn't be worth it. That's why I decided to let you go. To let you be free of me."

My eyes are burning, and it's not just because the lights are so bright. During this pause, there is pin drop silence.

"The mistake I made was that I never asked if that's what you wanted. I never asked. I just assumed. I was a coward. The stuff they wrote about you; I took it personally. I made it all about *me*. I shouldn't have. It always should have been about you first. I'm so sorry, Lily!"

As I carry on talking about her, about us, I feel a little bit like my old self again. I feel my old energy return. I feel lighter. It's like I can feel her presence. I can feel her forgiveness.

"So, I want you to know I'll grovel and beg. I'll take it all back and try harder. I'll put in the work every single day to become the kind of man who deserves your company and affection. I can't express how sorry I am for how everything went down. Know, please, that I never believed them. I was trying to protect you from *them* as well as myself. Because I'm just a fuck-up. Forty years old and twice divorced like the banner above the stage says. I don't deserve you, but if you choose to forgive me, I'll cherish you for as long as I live."

It makes no sense, but as I carry on talking, I just

know that coming out here tonight and starting my set in the most unorthodox way ever—without telling a single joke—was exactly the right thing to do. And that gives me the confidence to pivot as I get up off my seat, grab the microphone out of its stand, and address the audience directly again.

"Now, who's ready to hear some jokes?"

It takes half a second or so for the first person to start clapping. Then, more join in, until finally the whole theater is on its feet, giving me a standing ovation. I'd like to think the applause is for Lily rather than for me. And so, I make good on my promise, and actually tell some jokes until time's up.

* Lily *

I still can't believe Claire got me a ticket to watch tonight. Jill told me when I first joined that she's an excellent boss to work for, even if she can be aloof at times. She was right. I've only been a part of the crew for a few weeks, and I already feel at home.

The seat she got me isn't quite in the front row, but close enough—one of the VIP rows reserved for the network. As a result, the others are taken up by vaguely familiar faces I don't have the mental capacity to identify right now. I think I see a couple of daytime TV actors, news anchors, and other comedians on either side of me. Mom would be beside herself with excitement if she knew. I'm definitely not going to tell her, or I'll never hear the end of why I didn't get autographs.

I'm so nervous by now, I can barely concentrate on what's going on, anyway. I hear only bits of the announcement introducing Sean on stage. I'm stunned in my seat by the resulting applause, and forget to clap at all.

Will Sean spot me from up there? I'm not sure how I would feel about that. I didn't come here to distract him or ruin his show with my presence. I just really needed to *see* him.

The audience is still applauding when he emerges, and I forget to breathe. It's a shock, being in his presence again. Even if it's one-sided and far off. My chest swells with a confusing mixture of emotions.

Heartache, regret, blind panic… But mostly, I'm also just really glad to be here. While I have no way of knowing how this is going to play out, something tells me it's a good thing I've taken the chance.

Sean greets the audience and starts to speak. I can only hear bits and pieces of what he's saying through the racing thoughts that overwhelm my mind. Until I hear my name.

"Lily…" said in just the same way he would say my name when we were alone.

It makes me feel called out and vulnerable. I look around to my left and right, but nobody else seems to realize that Sean is talking about *me*. *To me.*

Lily… It's like his voice is echoing in my mind. I press my lips together and all but hold my breath while I listen to Sean as he keeps rambling like a mad man. Ranting at the media. Being so damn hard on himself as usual.

Confessing… confessing that he loves me.

I'm frozen in my seat, and the whole room seems to be spinning around me. I can't look away. I can't get up. I can hardly breathe or do a damn thing anymore. All I can do is hold on tight to the armrests of my seat until my knuckles turn white, and wait for the roller coaster ride to be over.

The intro about the two of us and our relationship must have taken less than ten minutes out of the entire set, but I'm only just finding my bearings again after the show is nearly over.

"Before I go tonight, I want you all to know I almost didn't do this show tonight," Sean says. "Very nearly didn't. But my manager wanted his cut, and I had some parking fines to pay for, so…"

The people on either side of me chuckle. All I can do is stare at him.

"And I figured I'd do it for Lily. She's never asked me for a damn thing, you know? Nothing. I figured she deserved to know how I feel. Tonight's show is dedicated to her."

People all over start to applaud. Although I sat

through the last standing ovation because I was too stunned to react, this time I'm the first and only one to jump out of my seat.

I don't know what possesses me, but without thinking too much about it, I cup my hands around my mouth and shout his name as loud as I can. "Sean!"

He takes a couple of steps forward to the edge of the stage and spots me in the crowd. The look on his face is everything.

"Sean, I love you!" I scream.

"Holy shit, that's Lily," someone whispers behind me. Just like that, murmurs spread across the whole theater, until my name seems to be on everyone's lips.

Sean drops the microphone and climbs off the edge of the stage. Meanwhile, I try to push my way past the people seated next to me and rush to the front until we finally meet, just between the stage and the first row of seats. As the crowd behind me goes wild, applauding and whistling, I only have eyes and ears for Sean.

Here he is, right in front of me at last.

"Shit, I had no idea you'd be here," Sean says.

I try to sniffle the tears away. "Neither did I, until a very kind person gave me a ticket—it's a long story."

A couple of security guards surround us and escort us away, while the audience carries on whooping and applauding. Sean puts his arm protectively around my back. The gesture makes my knees go weak. It's okay though, because he won't let me fall.

The noise from the audience is deafening until we're out of sight. There behind the curtain, we finally get a moment of privacy. Not that that makes our reunion any less awkward. Now that he's right in front of me, suddenly I'm not sure what to say anymore. All I can do is stare into his eyes as he stares into mine. He still has the kindest eyes.

"It seems that we both have some issues," I remark finally.

"By the suitcase-full," he says.

"You realize that you could just get some therapy rather than unload all that stuff on your audience?" I tease.

He chuckles softly.

"I wish you'd talked to me sooner," I whisper.

"I didn't know how… How to say what I wanted to say, or how you'd take it. Will you ever forgive me?"

The look in his eyes isn't just remorseful, it's heartbreaking.

"It never occurred to me not to," I say.

Then, I stand up on my tippy toes, wrap my arms around him, and kiss him on the lips. Such glorious relief. All the pent up emotions from the last month or so rattle free and wreak havoc in my body and soul. I don't know whether to laugh or cry. To hug him, kiss him, or run away and hide.

I can't let go, and it seems, neither can he. We cling to each other, as if it's this one hug or kiss that will sustain us for the rest of our lives.

When Claire offered me the ticket, I had no idea how tonight would turn out. But I had to take a chance. Because even though technically Sean and I have been apart much longer than we were ever together, neither of us could deal very well with being apart.

His crazy performance made that very clear—at least to me. And I've been hopelessly adrift ever since the day he left as well. Maybe all the pain was necessary. We're different people now after everything we went through. We've learned from our mistakes, hopefully.

Thinking back to all he said on stage—how he saw me, when I did nothing but beat myself up for being a useless fuck-up… It's going to take a while for all of it to sink in, but I'm sure now that the floodgates are open and we're able to talk freely, he'll be there to remind me. Just as I'll be there to remind him of everything he is to me.

This terrible experience will only make us stronger. Failure is no longer an option.

EPILOGUE

*** Lily ***

Three Months Later.

I wake up next to Sean, just like I have so many times before. The experience hasn't gotten old, though. Something tells me it never will.

The flat on St. James's Park, with its large, airy rooms and beautiful furnishings, continues to impress, though I've become a lot better about considering it 'home'. And of course, there's the man himself, who looks at peace beside me. His presence fills me with a sense of warmth and belonging I've never felt before.

Because I'm his. And he's mine. And nothing will ever stand in the way of that ever again. Least of all our own insecurities, our own baggage.

Ours is the family I've always strived to create, though it's going to be just the two of us for now. We'll wait a few years until my career settles down before thinking of children… Plus, I get to practice first by playing aunt to Alexis' little baby once it arrives just before Christmas.

Today, it's Sean's long-awaited day off from shooting. And it so happens that I'm in between projects too. The dating show Jill hired me on led to a bunch more offers for me, and the next one is just around the corner.

Just how we'll spend the day, I'm not sure yet. But I know it's going to be another Awesome Day Off. This time, it won't matter how many photographers follow us. The secret is out. Ever since Sean's show aired, we both feel lighter and more comfortable in our own skins.

Funnily, the scathing criticisms and harsh judgments in the press have reduced just as our relationship has become stronger. Sean's public declaration of love for me won over the audience, and the media had to follow suit. Tearing us down simply didn't sell enough papers and magazines for them anymore. And even if they hadn't stopped—fuck them, like Sean said that night. As long as things are right between the two of us, I couldn't give a toss what anyone else thinks. Nobody can hurt us anymore.

Sean starts to stir, his eyes opening as he turns onto his side and wraps his arm around me.

"Morning, beautiful," he says.

This is how he's been greeting me. Every morning, for the past three months. It never ceases to make me smile.

"Morning, handsome," I reply.

He always makes a face when I say that, but I know deep down he likes it. Because he can see in my eyes that I mean it.

"Happy day off! What would you like to do today?" I ask.

He stretches out his arms and shoulders, then hugs me tight again. I love this part of our mornings together. How we just can't get enough of each other.

"I have a few ideas."

"You're pretty insatiable for an old man," I tease. Not that I'd ever complain.

"All your fault! I mean, look at you!"

He starts kissing my neck, which gives me shivers and feels so very good all at the same time. This is always the point of no return. Not that I could ever resist when he looks at me *that way*. And once the neck kisses start, he always has me purring like a kitten. I'm still not so great at the delayed gratification thing…

Unlike the quickies we share early on working days, I already know we're going to take things slow this morning. With nowhere to be all day, we have all the time in the world to dedicate to each other.

Sean climbs on top of me and cups one hand behind my neck, using the other to slip the strap of my nightie off my shoulder. I love how big and strong he feels on top of me. A real man. *My* man.

I wrap my arms all around him and hold him tight. This is the best way to start the day; every day.

Sean continues to kiss and nibble on my neck,

while exploring the rest of my body with his free hand. He knows just how and where to touch me to drive me crazy. The man plays me like a fiddle. My partner in crime; my love. Forever.

I wiggle my thighs apart to give him free access to every part of me. Whatever he wants, whenever he wants it. I'm his to play with and he knows it. I can never get enough of him and the crazy, off-the-charts chemistry we share.

He slips his hand in between us and starts to tease me. First, he caresses my lips, dipping his finger into my depths to coat them in my wetness. Then he flicks just the tip of it across my clitoris. It's intense enough to make me squeal. I love it.

My body tingles and hums all over. Only he can tune into my frequency to make me resonate with pleasure.

He knows how to modulate his touch. How to stimulate just enough to edge me closer to orgasm, without overdoing it and cutting the experience too short.

Sean is by far the most patient lover I've ever had. A god between the sheets, though he'll never believe it no matter how many times I tell him.

Just when I start to feel that familiar warmth in my lower abdomen, the early warning signs of my impending orgasm, he adjusts himself and enters me. Just the tip.

It's too much and yet not enough. He just stays there, teasing me further. And because he's weighing me down into the plush mattress, I can't even scratch this itch by moving much myself.

He knows exactly what this does to me. This is one of those mornings when he wants me to beg. And I'm not going to be shy about it either.

"Baby, I need you," I moan.

"Do you?"

"Sean, I need *all you've got.*"

He inches down a little, pushing into me halfway. It's impressive, the amount of self control he has. I don't. I'm still not very good at the whole delayed gratification thing, especially not when it comes to sex.

But as desperate as I am for him to take me already, I know the wait will be worth it. I've never had trouble reaching orgasm, especially not with Sean. But when he really takes his time and stretches things out, the pleasure I feel is off the charts.

And so I try to grit my teeth and stop badgering him already. My fingers dig deeply into his ass and back, no doubt leaving imprints and perhaps even scratches. He doesn't mind it. In fact, I've come to realize he enjoys a bit of pain.

I keep exploring his body with my fingernails, grabbing a handful of love handle along the way. I love that he's chunky. I have plenty to hang on to when we make love.

He shudders underneath my touch. It's the only sign I'm getting that my arousal is getting to him as well. He isn't as unaffected and in control as he's pretending to be.

Ever so slowly, he starts to lower himself further down until he's all the way in. Then he pauses again. It's a beautiful sort of agony.

I tighten up my pelvis, allowing me to feel his whole length inside of me. He's so big, stretching me out even though he's not doing much at all. *Yet.*

Still, I can feel the pressure inside of me growing. Tighten. Release. Tighten. Release. I knew those Kegel exercises would come in handy. Salvation is in sight and I cannot wait.

His breaths start to quicken. Little shudders pass through the muscles in his shoulders and back. The cracks in his resolve are starting to show as well. I know I've almost won.

Finally, he joins in, pulling away and pushing into me in smooth strokes. The change of pace momentarily pulls me off the precipice of my release.

"Not yet, sweetheart," he whispers in my ear.

He's trying, bless him. He's trying to stretch things out, but I can hear the same desperation in his voice which I've felt right from the start. He's close too; he always is in the morning.

Instead of speeding up, he slows down, angling his

hips just so to grind his whole length against my vulva on the way in and out. That does it for me every time.

Just as my climax tends to do it for him. I cry out his name and dig my fingernails in hard once again. Butterflies fill my entire chest cavity. My skin heats and cools at the same time, as waves of relief wash over me.

"Sean! Oh my God!"

His whole body tightens, but he still keeps the pace. In and out, ever so slowly. Sweat starts to collect on his brow. His eyes are half-closed and his lips pressed together into a tight, straight line. The same frown I've seen so many times before starts to deepen above me.

I'm filled with a heat I wouldn't know how to live without anymore. I'm hopelessly addicted to this sweet torture and the antidote which only he can provide. Because I'm still riding my orgasm. Still overcome with pleasure, for as long as he stays buried inside of me.

Finally, he does increase his rhythm. While I fall apart underneath him, overcome by sensations I would have never felt if not for his skillful manipulations, he speeds up ever faster and finishes inside of me moments later.

We pause here, gasping for air while he scoops me up in his arms and rests his forehead against mine.

"Lily," he whispers, as soon as he's caught his

breath somewhat.

I smile and lean up to kiss him on the tip of his nose.

"Lily, I love you."

I'll never tire of hearing him say these words. Just as I'll never tire of saying them to him.

"I love you too."

Ever since the first time he's said it, up on that stage for the world to see and hear, he's been telling me at every possible opportunity. And I've been telling him at least as often.

"Lily," he says, raising himself and looking down into my eyes.

"Yes?"

"I know what I want to do today. On our day off… Only if you agree, of course."

"What's that?" I ask.

"Ring shopping."

I frown and want to ask what he's talking about. He looks serious and solemn, which is unusual for him. It takes a second for the penny to drop.

"Will you marry me, Lily?"

I stare up at him in shock. "Sean! Oh my God!"

"You don't have to. I just thought…" he whispers.

I shake my head. It's a rare occurrence, but the old Sean from early in our relationship has made an appearance. The Sean who wasn't quite sure what I was doing with him in the first place. "I know I don't *have* to. But…"

He waits for my answer with a most disarming little frown on his face. It's adorable.

"Of course! Yes! I *want* to!" I exclaim.

Tears sting in my eyes and I can't stop smiling.

Neither can he. And so we keep grinning at each other like idiots for a few seconds. Or maybe hours. Time has slowed to a crawl. The only sound in the room is the insane thumping of my heart, which is just about ready to burst out of my chest.

Until I wrap my arms tightly around his neck, and pull him down into me for a kiss to remember. Our first kiss as an engaged couple.

I can't wait to tell Alexis about this. And Jill. And maybe even my mom and Claire as well. Hell, I'll take out a full page ad in the *Times* to tell the whole world, that's how excited I am.

We'd obviously discussed our expectations for the future already, that same night after his show. We stayed up all night just talking. Okay, talking and making out. And having sex. And talking…

We're already committed to each other. All in. But with his history, I didn't think he'd want to take this step. Not this soon, and maybe not ever. I guess this is a sign then. We're truly ready to leave our past behind and jump headfirst into our future.

Mr. and Mrs. Cleary, or: 'Cleary Family', like the nameplate outside this flat already reads. For better or for worse. Now and forever.

Our relatively short relationship might have taken us through some ups and downs already, but we're only just getting started. We'll love each other and support each other and be there for each other for the rest of our lives.

I cannot wait.

AUTHOR'S NOTE

Thanks so much for reading *All My Heart!*

Perhaps you've been following me for a while, perhaps you're new to my work. But now that you're here, I'd like to give you a little background on how this book came to be...

My writing career started all the way back in October 2012 when I took a very deep breath, closed my eyes, crossed my fingers and even my toes and clicked 'Publish' on my first short story. That steamy little piece called *Ladies' Day*, and the book it grew into eventually (Beautiful Stranger) are still relevant today because it features a curvy heroine and her more mature lover. It serves as my first foray into steamy body positive romance.

Since then, I've published a whole bunch of books, in various romance sub genres; as L. Moone I write contemporary, and as Lorelei Moone I write about shifters, vampires and other paranormals. Certain themes tend to repeat themselves throughout my catalogue.

Beauty lies in the eye of the beholder. The hang-ups we tend to have about ourselves and our bodies often aren't shared by the opposite sex. While it's a lot more popular to write about gorgeous curvy ladies and their athletic admirers than the other way around, I've dabbled in both in the past. I just never felt there was a big market for husky men in romance (my sales numbers supported this notion, unfortunately). 2020 changed that thanks to Jessa Kane and her sexy big boy titles, *Hefty* and *Husky*. My mind was blown, and I absolutely devoured them and couldn't get enough. I'm slowly seeing other authors enter this space, so perhaps the time has come? I hope so, because I'd love to write (and read!) a whole bunch more of these...

The idea for *All My Heart* came about while I was still writing book 1 in the *Husky Men Do It Better* series, *Recipe for Passion*. I was almost done with that book when inspiration struck me for something completely different. As much as I wanted my thoughts to revolve around the ending of that book, I had this entire scenario in my head of an age gap romance in which the hero is a stand-up comedian, and the heroine initially has no idea who he is and the two share absolutely crazy chemistry from their first meeting onwards, but also have a lot of hang-ups about themselves and their budding relationship.

I did in fact start writing this book then, because the muse just wouldn't shut up about it. I just had no idea whatsoever how to fit it into the series, so I wrote *Best Friends Forever* next which stars Jill in the lead role. And *All My Heart*, the way that it started at least, didn't fit in anywhere at all. I didn't even know how to involve any of the existing characters in the series! Finally, once I realized that Lily needs a job, and Jill's intern quits part of the way through shooting *Sealed with a Kiss*, I had found my connection and the book ended up becoming a spin-off from the *Husky Men* series, entering a series of its own; *Husky Ever After*.

By the way, if you've read more of my work, you'll also find that *All My Heart* serves as a cross-over into another series of mine; *Coffee & Curves*. Lily's cousin, Alexis, is actually the subject of the fourth title in that series (*One Night with my Boss*).

But, enough of all that. If you're like me and you just can't wait to read more dad bod titles, you'll be pleased to know that I have a whole bunch of titles out in a similar vein. Check out the rest of the *Husky Ever After* series, as well as *Husky Men Do It Better*.

And that's enough from me. I hope you enjoyed the story as much as I did while writing it, and if you're interested in reading more of my work, perhaps you'll consider signing up for my newsletter. I'll even give you a free story when you sign up.

x, Lorelei

FIND ME AT:

- ❖ LMoone.com
- ❖ Lorelei Moone on Facebook
- ❖ AuthorLMoone on Instagram

I also write Paranormal Romance as Lorelei Moone. Check out LoreleiMoone.com for more information.

SPECIAL OFFER!

For a limited time, all new mailing list subscribers will receive a FREE short story, called At First Sight.

Claim your free copy here:

LMoone.com
Look for the newsletter sign-up form at the bottom of the page.